THE CONTRACTOR

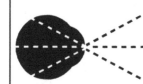

This Large Print Book carries the Seal of Approval of N.A.V.H.

THE CONTRACTOR

JAMES C. WORK

THORNDIKE PRESS
A part of Gale, a Cengage Company

GALE
A Cengage Company

Farmington Hills, Mich • San Francisco • New York • Waterville, Maine
Meriden, Conn • Mason, Ohio • Chicago

Thorndike Press® Large Print Western.
The text of this Large Print edition is unabridged.
Other aspects of the book may vary from the original edition.
Set in 16 pt. Plantin.

LIBRARY OF CONGRESS CATALOGING-IN-PUBLICATION DATA

Names: Work, James C., author.
Title: The contractor / by James C. Work.
Description: Large print edition. | Waterville, Maine : Thorndike Press, a part of
   Gale, Cengage Learning, 2017. | Series: Thorndike Press large print western
Identifiers: LCCN 2017017814| ISBN 9781432839345 (hardcover) | ISBN 1432839349
   (hardcover)
Subjects: LCSH: Large type books. | BISAC: FICTION / Westerns. | FICTION /
   Historical. | GSAFD: Western stories.
Classification: LCC PS3573.O6925 C66 2017 | DDC 813/.54—dc23
LC record available at https://lccn.loc.gov/2017017814

Published in 2017 by arrangement with James C. Work

Printed in Mexico
1 2 3 4 5 6 7 21 20 19 18 17

ACKNOWLEDGMENT

Inspiration for the character of Detective N. K. Boswell in this narrative comes from *Hands Up, or Twenty Years of Detective Life in the Mountains and on the Plains (Reminiscences by General D. J. Cook, Rocky Mountain Detective Association)* by General David J. Cook. Published by The Narrative Press, Santa Barbara, California, 2001.

FOREWORD
BY PHILLIP PIERCE, REPORTER

It was in 1868 that I first heard of N. K. Boswell, the legendary detective of the American West. You might say I was knocking around Omaha — my daily routine was to go knocking on editors' doors looking for work. An unemployed newspaper reporter could eke out a meager living by finding stories, writing them up, then carrying them to one of the several newspapers to sell them to whichever editor might be interested. A financial page editor, for instance, might buy a story about the arrival of a new bank vault. The man and wife who published a small biweekly might buy a story about the opening of a new mercantile store.

News stories lay in every direction in that city, from the progress of civic improvements to the coming of new businesses and from the army activity at Fort Dodge to the railroad's plans to span the Missouri with a railroad bridge. And, of course, there were the many accidents and confrontations that accompanied a city as it struggled to grow into its new identity. As it grew, Omaha was acquiring a reputation for rowdyism. The men who came to build the roads and bridges, who came to lay the rails and dig the foundations, they were of the rough and ready variety. They required rough and ready entertainment, the sort of after-work relaxation in which fights were likely to break out. All it took was one tired railroad man drinking up the last of his wages and having his arm jostled by a bricklayer next to him. Almost every night saw a brawl in one of the liquor joints or dance halls on Front Street where the stockyard bullies, railroad hunkies and construction crews were apt to gather.

"Reckon I got a story in mind. I could assign you to it," said the editor of a small weekly. "Pay you by the inch, leave the door open to a follow-up."

He looked me up and down with extravagant slowness.

"Thing is," he continued, "I ain't sure you'd survive it. You don't carry much weight on those bones. Judgin' from that pretty nose of yours and those piano player hands, I'd say you ain't never been punched in the face nor punched anybody yourself.

Ever been in a fistfight, have you?"

"No, sir," I confessed.

"This story, it's about fire hazards down along the river. The way I heard it, all the way from the ferry landing on down past the stockyards there's nothin' but ramshackle cribs and lean-tos just waitin' for a fire to break out. Need somebody to interview the fire brigade captain, but mostly to go down along the river and get personal opinions from the citizens down there. Some of them boys would rob you just to get that Tattersall vest or them new boots. Some would like to get you in a fight just 'cause you look so clean and fresh."

"Well . . . ," I said.

I straightened my shoulders and spine, trying to look tough and resolute.

"I need the money," I said. "Got a job waiting for me in Cheyenne, but I need train fare and money for food."

He looked at me and shook his head as if to say, "What sort of fools are they sending west these days?" Then with an audible sigh he scribbled on a piece of paper and put it in my hand. He escorted me to the door.

"There's the name of the fire brigade captain. Your deadline's Thursday for the next week's edition. Don't get hurt. Stay out of fights."

■ ■ ■ ■

Despite his advice, that very same afternoon, I managed to walk into a serious fracas without half trying. The fire captain had pointed me toward a particularly large and noisy "dance" hall where very little dancing took place but there was a great deal of drinking, arguing, and socializing with the ladies of the line who worked there.

"We keep a close eye on that building," he told me. "There's a wagonload of oil lamps and candles in the place. And there's little nooks around the dance floor with curtains. And usually too many people at a time. Dry wood, oiled floors, everything you need for a good bonfire."

Although it was broad daylight outside, when I pushed through the doors of the place, I had to stand a minute to let my eyes adjust to the gloom. I was at the top of three steps that led down to the dance floor and felt pretty conspicuous standing there. Fortunately a fistfight was just getting underway, which meant that nobody took much notice of a skinny young fellow in a Tattersall vest and plug hat. No blows had been thrown as yet; a brawny brawler with hips like a cat and shoulders broad enough that he could lean simultaneously on both sides of a doorway was circling a hugely fat tough who was turning to keep track of his tormentor.

Words were being exchanged in two heavy dialects. One sounded something like German and the other had a smack of old Ireland to it, both seriously slurred by alcohol and anger. The audience egged them on with shouts of encouragement and laughter.

"Five dollars on Riley!" someone shouted.

For a moment the contest was a standoff; then the brawler got careless and danced too close to the fat man. A fist the size of a holiday ham shot out like a bolt of lightning and caught him full in the face. He replied with a haymaker of his own, a roundhouse blow that could snap a porch post in half; this was nonchalantly absorbed by the fat man, who made another ham-fisted punch and connected with the dancer's chest.

Another heavy punch, then another roundhouse, the crowd cheering each thud and grunt. The slugging contest continued until someone behind the fat man grabbed his belt, whereupon the thing deteriorated into a general brawl. One of the fat man's friends took exception to any attempt to hinder him and expressed his opinion of the grabber's poor sportsmanship by smashing a beer bottle down on his skull. The dancing pugilist then danced into a puddle of spilled beer and went down with a thud, whereupon somebody put a boot into him, whereupon someone else threw a kidney punch into the kicker. Where there had been shouts of encouragement and general hilarity, now there were war cries and fierce shouts and a general angry roar. I remained as still as a mouse in the dubious protection of the doorway. But everyone else in the place, including the prostitutes and bartenders, seemed to be involved in pushing and pulling and throwing awkward punches in all directions.

Behind me the door opened, letting in a glaring flood of afternoon sunshine. It was the fire brigade captain in his red flannel shirt and red braces, and now he was wearing his official black fire helmet with a big brass badge on the front. Recognizing me, he looked at the battling, screaming crowd and smiled.

"Getting a good story?" he shouted.

"My interviews aren't going very well," I shouted back.

"We need to break this up before somebody tips over a lantern and starts a fire.

Place would go up like a box of tinder sticks."

"We?"

I could see he was unarmed except for a small belt ax. He looked in fine trim, and he had thirty or more pounds on me, but that wasn't saying much. What I couldn't see was how he intended to stop the fight all by himself: I had already decided he was using the word "we" in the royal or editorial sense.

Like a man going to work, he walked down the steps and into the heart of the melee. With great gentleness he carefully urged this man and that man out of his way, much as you might do on a crowded sidewalk, until he came to the panting fat man and the bruised Irishman. And then the most amazing thing happened.

Drawing close to the two fighters, the brigade captain raised his right fist with two fingers extended. He looked from one man to the other but otherwise was motionless, just standing there with his arm in the air and two fingers pointing at the ceiling.

The big Irishman's brow furrowed into a scowl that would scare the gargoyles off Saint Pat's cathedral. In the light of the overhead lamps I saw the scowl gradually give way to something resembling comprehension and then his own massive arm haltingly rose, two fingers extended, aping the gesture of the fire captain. A bystander nearby took up the signal next, then four or five others. I saw hands going up all over the place, like an ocean wave emanating from the center outward, followed by a hushing of the ruckus. The quiet simply spread out until everyone was quiet. Even the piano player gave over trying to play accompaniment to the riot and sat at his keyboard like an admonished pupil.

The fire captain stepped up to the bartender and said something I could not hear, then returned to where I was standing.

"That seems to be the end of it," he said. "I mentioned to the barman that it might be less expensive to buy everyone a drink than to replace the furniture."

We went out together. The late sun was dazzlingly bright, and even the odor of the riverside stockyards seemed fresh and clean compared to the stale beer and tobacco smell of the dance hall.

"How did you do that?" I asked. "That hand in the air trick?"

"Learned it from a lawman," the captain replied. "Ever hear of N. K. Boswell? I deputied for him a while. Saw him use that trick any number of times. Mostly in saloons, with cowboys. He did it with a lynch mob once, but they weren't all that enthusiastic about the lynching to begin with. Mind you, with a really determined gang he had to face down, Boswell would draw on the leaders. He didn't fool around, that was his reputation. That, and being a dead shot."

"Can't say I ever heard of him," I said.

"Hang around places like that one back there, you'll hear the toughs talk about him. Or else travel around Kansas Territory, and you'll hear about him. Being a reporter, if you were to shadow Boswell you'd get more stories than you had time to write down. Like I told you, he taught me the trick of staying calm and quiet, and it has served me well in doing my job."

As I said, that was in 1868. I was young and my only assets consisted of an innocent, freshly scrubbed face and two years' journalism experience. These were my tools for conquering the West, together with a spare shirt and a letter from a Wyoming newspaper promising me a job. "If you can get here."

I got as far as Omaha, where I ran out of funds. But by sleeping rough a few nights and living on nickel plates of beans, I survived until I had hunted up enough piecemeal work to pay for a cheap room. A couple of more weeks of it and I had enough money for a train ticket to Cheyenne. As I said, I was ambitious to be a reporter. Even during the long train ride across the Nebraska prairie to Wyoming, I interviewed passengers in hopes of finding a good human-interest story among them.

The crusty editor of the Cheyenne *Leader* newspaper was indeed surprised that I had actually arrived. And he was happy enough to see me, for he happened to be in need of a correspondent, preferably one who didn't require much in the way of salary and who was expendable enough to send into harm's way. Unlike that editor back in Omaha, the *Leader*'s man expressed absolutely no reservations about my unimposing stature and my youth. Seeing that I was eager to go, he offered me a railroad pass and a month's pay in advance. My assignment would be to travel west along the rails of the Union Pacific, still under construction.

"Take the train all the way west to the end of track," he said, "it's somewhere out there in that godforsaken sagebrush desert they call Wyoming — I don't think even God knows why they call it 'Wyoming' — and send me back reports on the progress of the almighty Union Pacific enterprise. I understand that pretty soon they'll have 'er linked up and connect the whole country. Coast to coast. That's your story. Send back news about how far they got, who the important men are, what about the Indians — that kind of stuff."

In my youthful idealism I pictured myself posing atop a rocky promontory, cutting a romantic figure in wide-brimmed hat and riding boots, my pencil poised over my notebook. In the valley at my feet would be an army of America's finest men, clean and handsome lads laying the steel rails of a transcontinental railroad to carry the inexorable and inevitable progress of civilization westward. I would write about the wonderful machines, the miracle of blasting powder and steam engines making a straight path through the empty wilderness, and I would write the stories of the American workingman, his hopes and dreams, the sweethearts he left behind, the joy of laboring with sledgehammer and shovel.

That was the daydream.

In reality, I was to find myself in a smelly, rough town crammed with crude men from all corners of the globe, a place where the constant clatter and racket of construction was punctuated with vicious swearing in a dozen strange languages. Rather than standing on a breezy, bucolic vantage point, I would spend my days walking dirt streets that became ankle-deep mud when it rained and waist-deep dust when it did not.

Armed with my railroad pass and month's advance wages I boarded the westbound cars. An unshaven conductor chewing on an unlit cigar informed me that the end of the track was now located at Fort Steele, halfway through the Wyoming Territory. The train started with a rude jerk that slammed me back into my seat hard enough to nearly snap my neck and, after what seemed like endless hours of swaying and bumping and listening to my stomach growl, I was grateful to see solid ground when I stepped off the cars. From the crude rail station I walked into the most dangerous, most lawless, most ungovernable collection of ruffians since the predations of Genghis Khan.

I also walked into my first big news story, a drama of senseless murder and incredible courage and perseverance. My report of this incredible killing was given no more than two inches of print in the Cheyenne *Leader*. However, the saga of the ensuing pursuit of the murderer by Detective Boswell would ultimately fill two of my journals from cover to cover.

CHAPTER 1

I got wind of the story within a few days of my arrival in Fort Steele. It was the kind of human-interest piece that would engage the readers of the Cheyenne *Leader,* involving the dramatic and bloody murder of Charlie Madalone. The victim was an engaging and perpetually cheerful youth who had come up from Colorado to find work with the railroad. Being of slight build, he was not suited for heavy labor. But he was good with animals and was hired by one of the contractors, Mr. Kane Kelly, as night herder for the railroad's stock of draught horses, mules and beef cattle.

The herding job with Mr. Kelly's company suited Charlie well. His principal possession — indeed, the only thing of value that he owned — was an excellent cow pony. According to men I interviewed afterward, young Charlie liked nothing better than to be mounted on his cherished pony, riding

19

gently around the draught herd and singing or whistling the old tunes. There were times, they said, when Charlie missed his home in Colorado and spoke of returning; for the most part, however, he was contented with riding through the starlit nights and sleeping through the heat of day.

And then one evening he came to work and found his cow pony missing.

Some men thought that the pony had wandered away and they helped Charlie search the outlying hills and draws, but to no avail. They watched for signs of predators in case a bear or mountain lion had taken the animal and still found nothing. They all felt very sorry for Charlie and tried to help in any way they could, but eventually they were forced to admit that his pony was probably stolen by a band of young Cheyenne Indians. They had been known to raid the railroad's livestock for beef cattle and riding horses.

Whoever was guilty, the fact was that Charlie's beloved friend and prized possession was gone and could not be recovered. Another mount was provided for him and he went back to night herding, but he was a lad much changed. Now he went about town with his head drooping. When people tried to smile at him, he met them with a grim, sad face, finding neither joy nor comfort in life. He went to the army post for help, to see if they could send a patrol to look for whomever had stolen his horse, but he was told that they had no way of knowing where to look, nor did they have the manpower to spare on such a mission. The local law was of even less help, since it consisted of one constable and a part-time deputy whose main duty was to guard the drunks in the small jail and take care of stray dogs.

As I said, the railroad laborers who knew Charlie all liked him and tried their best to console him for his loss. They were a tough and hard-shelled lot. Beneath their rough exteriors, however, they still had human hearts and felt deep sympathy for the gentle kid. Many regarded Charlie as they would a kid brother or son who had been robbed of the only thing of value he really owned. They talked about his loss around their cooking fires in the evenings. And being men of resolution, men of action, it was not long before they came up with a plan to help Charlie.

I interviewed several of the men afterward. None of them seemed to know who had first come up with the plan, although each of them had his own theory about it.

"Oh," one said, "no doubt it was Johnson. He's that kind of man, you know. Give you the shirt from his back. It was definitely him who started it."

Someone else theorized that McIntosh was the instigator. Another thought it must have been the fireman Underhill, but the fact was that no one could definitely prove who started it. In any event, on the next payday someone took one of the canvas pails used to carry railroad spikes and painted the name "Charlie" on it. The Charlie pail went up and down the tracks at the work site and appeared in the saloons. It was passed from hand to hand as the men came out of the paymaster's shack, each man tossing in a bit or two. And before you knew it, the Charlie pail had collected enough money to purchase a new cow pony for their little friend, and a new saddle rig besides.

Good horses and saddles were in short supply in Fort Steele. The livery stable usually had one or two mounts for sale, but these tended to be either old, lame or ornery. And as for saddles, the best place in town to buy one was the principal saloon where the bartender generally had one or two he had kept as collateral after lending money. The men in charge of the Charlie pail would need to ride the work train back to Cheyenne. Two of them volunteered to do just that, and when they returned they had with them a fine-looking, spirited pony to replace the one Charlie had lost. The boy was sadly overjoyed to have his own pony again, although it was not the same as the one he had lost, and he was deeply, deeply touched by his friends' generosity and concern.

Mr. Kane Kelly, the contractor, viewed these charitable proceedings with undisguised scorn. He regarded horses as brutes to be worked until they died in harness, nothing more. He knew that the wild wastes of Wyoming territory made a dangerous place for a man afoot, but he did not care. If the boy was unlucky or careless and lost his horse, that was just too bad. He could use a company horse for night guarding; his workmen had no business taking time off to get him another pony. The bookkeeper told me that Mr. Kelly had considered docking the pay of the two men who went to Cheyenne for Charlie's new pony. Instead, he took away their next three days off. The same bookkeeper said that Mr. Kelly stood in the office window glaring down at the cheering, laughing crowd of workmen as they presented the pony to Charlie. Not only were they wasting company time, they were wasting it on a boy who had never accomplished anything and who had nothing.

Kelly himself owned everything the men depended upon for their livelihood — horses included — and yet when he walked among them, he got no more recognition than a finger touched to a hat brim. But upon spotting Charlie coming in from his night duty the same men would wave and smile and greet him by name. Mr. Kelly paid them the very wages the men were so free with; but were *he* to lose something of value they would only say, among themselves, he could afford it.

I wrote up the story of Charlie's pony as a simple and straightforward tale of human generosity. The newspaper would keep it on file and use it to fill up a page somewhere. But I couldn't seem to leave it at that. Something about the situation nagged at me, and I continued interviewing the hunkies and gandy dancers and tie hacks. There was a great deal of human drama going on at this outpost of civilization, and I began to see a much more complicated picture behind the simple story of Charlie's pony.

First there was the stark contrast between the spirit of helping one another and caring for one another and the notion that in the frontier, it was every man for himself. Mr. Kelly, according to the men who labored for him, was guilty of being out for himself and himself only. They thought he was mean in both senses of the word: cruel and stingy. He was respected for his power, yes. Appreciated for the wages he paid, yes. Envied, sometimes, for his personal fortune, which was rumored to be in excess of a hundred thousand. But he was not liked. He lacked generosity. No, that wasn't quite correct. He could not *comprehend* generosity. The word had no meaning for him, which made him the object of conversation among the men.

On the frontier, you see, even the poorest hermit could be depended upon to share his crust of bread and his meager campfire with a needy stranger. It was a wide, terrible place where the very land itself seemed malevolent; each desert expanse, each frozen canyon seemed to set its face against humans. Men spoke of "winning" and "conquering" those open spaces, spoke of "taming" the West as if the place were a living, scheming being. It was because of this, I believe, that among the Irish and the Dutch, the Swedes and the Chinamen, there existed a silent camaraderie, an unspoken code under which a man was obliged to share his water, his weapon and his very welfare with any fellow in need.

Mr. Kane Kelly lacked this, and he lacked it entirely. Stingy and self-contained, he had no understanding of a man who would give something to another man unless there was a foreseeable profit in doing so.

I wrote up the story of Charlie's pony and posted it to Cheyenne. In due course it was published in the *Leader* and that was that. Little did I know at that point that there would be a second and much more sinister installment. A murder, in cold blood.

The murder took place while I was out of town: news came to Fort Steele that there had been a derailment about thirty miles back up the track in which men had been injured and a locomotive had gone off the tracks. As it happened, I had recently made the acquaintance of a photographer named Robert Platt, a young man like myself who had taken up residence at Fort Steele in hopes of making a photographic record of the "real West." To him it presented an opportunity to sell pictures of the accident to the newspapers. To me it simply seemed more interesting than anything happening in Fort Steele. We therefore made plans to go. And since it involved the transcontinental railroad, the main reason for my being in Wyoming, I telegraphed the newspaper editor, who agreed to pay expenses.

Robert and I hired a buggy and team, packed up some food and bedding for ourselves, and set out to investigate. It took us a day to drive to the scene of the accident, then a day to take photographs and interview the train crew. On the third day we drove back to Fort Steele, congratulating ourselves on getting an exclusive story and pictures. But we had no sooner arrived back in town when our celebratory mood was utterly quashed by the news that a tragedy had occurred in our absence.

Charlie Madalone had been murdered in cold blood.

Suddenly I found my job distasteful. I had to talk to anyone who knew anything about the incident. Over and over, I had to listen to the same gruesome details and opinions, trying to remain objective in order to gather the facts, while my informants were likely to be overcome with emotion as they described what they had seen. Or heard from others. The more they spoke about Charlie, the more I began to feel I had known him for a long time, that I had lost a good friend. I went about my investigation with grim and dogged determination, enduring a dozen strangers telling me repeatedly how the murder had happened.

Charlie Madalone, it seemed, had been seriously stricken with homesickness. The new pony had cheered him up, but the kindness of the men and the generosity of their act had the effect of awakening in Charlie a desire to be back among family and friends. He therefore resolved to return to his family in Colorado. And the idea of going home made him even more like the cheerful youngster the workmen had known, so his friends encouraged him to leave even though he would be greatly missed.

And so, one morning after the end of his shift, Charlie walked into Mr. Kelly's office, announced that he was quitting, and asked for the two months' wages that were owed to him. "That's damn short notice, boy," Kane Kelly grumbled. "I got a busy day already without trying to find a man to take the night guard. You'll stay."

"No, sir," Charlie replied. "I've made up my mind and packed my stuff. I'm going home."

"I'd rather you stay," Kane insisted. "Let's make it a week. Give me time to replace you."

"Patrick can take my shift tonight," Charlie argued. Patrick was the boy who watched the herd during the early morning hours.

"Look, boy! I told you it ain't convenient. Get out of here!"

"Mr. Kane, my mind's made up. Just let me have those two months' wages."

"All right," Kelly grumbled. "All right, take your damn wages and clear out. Can't stand a boy who argues back to me anyway. Bastard."

He turned to his bookkeeper, who later told me what happened.

"Give this kid his wages. But see that you deduct the price of that damned pony!"

"Wait!" Charlie said. "That pony was a gift to me from the men. To replace the one that was stole! You can't expect me to *pay* you for it! You don't understand."

"You're the one that don't understand. That's how business works. Look here, if you came to work and had your own shovel and you broke it I'd have to give you a new one. You couldn't work without it, could you? So why should I pay for it and make you a gift of it? I s'pose you'd expect to take my shovel with you when you quit, too."

"But those men, they bought that pony for me!"

"And where did they get the wages, and the time off they took, and the passes on the railroad to go get that damn animal? From the company, that's from where. It cost *me*. It didn't cost you. But you got it anyway. You can leave it here when you go, or the price comes out of your wages and that's final!"

Mr. Kelly remained intractable. He finally ordered Charlie to get out of his office, that he could take the wages he was offered or leave them on the table. The amount deducted for the pony was a considerable piece of money, especially to a boy who would not see employment for some time to come.

Leaving Kelly's office, young Charlie encountered some fellow workers. Wondering why he wasn't his cheerful self, they put arms over his shoulders and asked why he seemed so down in the mouth. He told them about the injustice done to him by Kelly and what Kelly had said to him. Angered, they not only urged him to press the matter, but spread the story abroad until everyone in that part of town was upset over the unfairness of the thing.

The next day, Charlie spotted Mr. Kelly walking toward the bank across the street and, with the support of a few friends, followed him into the bank. There he accosted Mr. Kelly in the presence of witnesses, demanding the money he was owed. Mr. Kelly flew into a rage. After much shouting and threatening, he stormed out of the bank yelling, "I'll fix you, you little son of a bitch, asking me for money!"

According to my informants, Mr. Kelly turned his back on Charlie and strode off toward his office. With slumped shoulders, Charlie went across the street to his pony. Minutes later, Kelly was seen coming along the opposite side of the street. And he was carrying a rifle.

Kelly stopped directly across from the boy, rested the rifle on a wagon wheel, took aim and shot Charlie where he stood.

"Oh! Mr. Kelly, you have shot me!" Charlie cried out as he fell. "Please! Let me live! I will not bother you again!"

Kelly was now walking across the street toward the boy, reloading his rifle as he came.

"No, I don't think you will," he said. "You'll never ask me for any money in a public bank again. I'll warrant you won't!"

And with those words he pulled the trigger to send a bullet crashing through the boy's skull.

Tom Johnson told me that a dozen or so men witnessed the act and were spellbound, unable to move as the sound of the shot faded and the smoke drifted away.

"None of us could believe it," Tom said. "One minute Charlie was standing there with his pony, and the next minute Mr. Kelly was standing over him aiming that rifle at his head. We couldn't move for the shock of it."

Those were the facts of the case as told to me. All of the witnesses to the barbaric act were on Kelly's payroll, like many of the civilians at Fort Steele, which is doubtlessly what prevented him from being lynched on the spot. Someone — I was unable to learn who it was — went for the town's constable, who came with two officers from the fort to arrest Kelly. He was locked up in the fort's guardhouse. However, on the night before I returned to Fort Steele, he somehow managed to escape. No one could give me any definite information about how he did it, although it was rumored that Kelly's brother and a couple of loyal employees had effected the contractor's departure from the guardhouse cell.

I managed to learn that Mr. Kelly's permanent address was in Council Bluffs, across the Missouri from Omaha; in Fort Steele it was generally believed that he had somehow stowed away on an eastbound train to Omaha and then had crossed over to Council Bluffs. This was borne out more than a month later, for word came that he had been arrested and jailed in Omaha. But once again he was able to escape. The theory was that someone was bribed to leave a cell door unlocked. Amazingly, from Omaha Mr. Kelly went straight home to Council Bluffs, where he was once again captured, jailed, and allowed to get away.

These reports angered Charlie's friends in Fort Steele, and even though I was still a relatively naive journalist, I knew enough to urge the men to discount these reports. For one thing, they arrived in Fort Steele in the form of abbreviated telegraph messages. The curt notes attached to my monthly instructions indicated that Kane Kelly was out of the picture: the contracting company went on as usual, operating under the leadership of Kane's brother, Clifton Kelly, and a rough band of hangers-on calling themselves "supervisors." They moved into Fort Steele and wasted no time in taking over Kane's office, bullying the railroad workers with abusive oaths and raised shillelaghs.

As for me, I dutifully kept on filing stories about the clever engineering of the Fort Steele Railway Bridge, improvements to the fort, arrivals of new citizens, and living conditions in general. It was not exciting work, and I was not the only one to think so; when I wrote about the town's plan for a new drinking-water well, my story was returned in the next mailbag. There was no note with it, only a pencil drawing showing a yawning editor.

CHAPTER 2

By 1869 Fort Steele had ceased to be an end-of-track railroad camp. Now it was just another dusty village with a few stores, a water tower for the trains and a small army garrison. The transcontinental railroad was completed, the ceremony at Promontory Point providing me with my last major news story, and 1870 found me back in Omaha and looking for work.

The Cheyenne *Leader* agreed to keep me on the payroll as a stringer, in case something newsworthy might happen in Omaha, and the fledgling *Omaha Daily Herald* similarly hired me as a stringer. Between those two jobs and doing dozens of freelance feature articles, I managed to pay for my room and board. It even paid for the shoe leather I wore out walking all over town in search of stories. Since I was young and eager — and possibly a bit naive — I seemed to find excitement in every aspect of this burgeoning city in the center of the plains. One day might see me perched on a corral rail at the sprawling Omaha stockyards writing about the latest shipments of cattle, while another day would take me downriver to write a feature about the grave of Sergeant Floyd, the only man to die on the Lewis and Clark Expedition. Or I would be sent to cover the dedication of a new church bell or the installation of a new undersheriff.

Two or three times a week I would walk down to the railroad yards and repair shops. The railroad was always a promising source of stories. The yards were like the hub of a wheel from which the rails went outward like spokes, some going upriver, some downriver, others angling toward the gold camps of Colorado. The men who worked on the locomotives or who loaded and unloaded the freight cars generally had bits of news for me. One day I was in the roundhouse listening to an engineer who was explaining the workings of a new kind of reciprocal steam valve. He happened to drop the name Kelly into the conversation.

"*Kane* Kelly, you mean?" I asked.

The engineer spat into the dust at our feet.

"The same," he snorted. "The tight-fisted bastard. Nearly cost us an engine, skimpin' on the spikes on that big curve just this side of the Elkhorn River. There's a story for you, the shoddy job they did on that stretch of track. Shoulda been twice as many sleepers on that curve. And double spikes. Double. Any worker worth his salt could see it. But the kinda cheap help Kelly hires don't know better. He even skimps on the ballast, and not just on the Elkhorn stretch but everywhere he goes. He gets away with usin' less crushed rock 'cause he fills in with sand or dirt and it don't hold the traffic. It's somethin' shameful."

"Wait a minute," I said. "Back up a little. Are you telling me that Kane Kelly is *still* contracting with the railroad?"

"I am. Can't say I know where he's workin' right at this minute, but I pray to the saints I never have to run a heavy engine down one of his tracks, that cheap bastard. They say he's bossing a crew out in the boondocks somewhere."

Now this *was* news! A murderer openly walking and working abroad. Once again I saw young Charlie's face before me and heard voices of sorrow in Fort Steele telling me the sad circumstances of Charlie's murder. And Kelly was back doing business as usual.

Suddenly all other stories became trivial.

That same morning I canvassed the railroad yards and repair shops until I had located two more railroad men who would verify that Kane Kelly was contracting again. I wrote the story without hesitation, boldly calling Kelly "the man who shot Charlie Madalone" and expressing my amazement that he was out of prison and acting as if nothing had happened. I sent it off to the Cheyenne *Leader* and waited eagerly to see it blazoned across the front page. But the editor apparently lacked my zeal for the discovery, because after several weeks he ran the story on an inside page beside the cattle prices and legal notices.

Nearly two months later a gentleman came knocking on my door at the boardinghouse. He was nicely dressed in suit and vest, wearing a bowler hat. He seemed neither old nor young, neither potbellied nor thin, but very muscular and fit.

"Mr. Pierce?" he said. "The one who writes for the Cheyenne *Leader*?"

He handed me his card. His handshake was like being gripped in an iron vise.

"I'm N. K. Boswell of Laramie City," he said. "Detective."

And there it was. The legend was standing on my threshold. As I said, in physique he looked quite fit but otherwise ordinary, neither short nor notably tall, neither thin nor heavy; but some indescribable aspect of his poise and bearing, some deep power in his eyes, told me he was a man who would have mastery of any social situation in which he found himself.

When I suggested we go into the boarding-house parlor to talk, he suggested that I get my coat and take a walk with him. I did so without hesitation.

"I will be direct and honest," he said, "and I expect the same from you. I saw your report in the Cheyenne *Leader* to the effect that Kane Kelly is free and abroad. When I asked the editor about it, he showed me an earlier article about the murder of one Charlie Madalone in Fort Steele. Neither story bore a byline, but the editor informed me they were written by a young reporter named Phillip Pierce. That is you."

Those eyes turned upon me as if daring me to deny it.

"True," I confessed. "You see, I was living in Fort Steele —"

"Good. I'm glad I have found you. I will tell you why I am interested in your stories, provided you agree to tell no one you have met me. I have nothing to hide, but I would prefer to have as few people as possible know about my presence in Omaha. Agreed?"

"Fine," I said. "Agreed."

"Very well," he said. "As I said earlier, my name is N. K. Boswell. I am with the Rocky Mountain Detective Association of Laramie City. Perhaps you've heard of General Cook, our founder and leader. The Association has offices and operatives in Denver, Kansas City and Saint Louis. Charlie Madalone's father has recently engaged us to look into his son's murder."

"I see," I said.

"You know this man Kelly," Mr. Boswell said.

"I have seen him, yes. I would recognize him if I saw him again. I would not say I know him, nor would I particularly care to."

"Good enough. Reporters keep notebooks, I assume."

"Yes."

"And your notebook would contain the names of those men whom you interviewed, the eyewitnesses to the murder?"

I swallowed hard and tried to disengage myself from his strong gaze.

"Yes," I said.

"I want that notebook," he continued. "I will engage a certified stenographer to copy the pertinent pages, which I will then post to my colleague at Laramie City. He will find those witnesses and collect depositions from them. I will return your notebook to you. We intend, you see, to build a watertight case against Kelly. I'm sure you will want to cooperate."

We walked on together. Thoughts swirled around in my mind like water going down a drain. Here was a fine news story, handed to me as if on a plate. Yet Boswell's request for secrecy was valid. As a journalist, I had a responsibility to report what I knew. I could image a long story, page one, with my byline, on the front of the *Herald.* Title, "Murderer Walks Among Us" screamer. And here was a well-respected detective hot on the trail of the killer, which made the story all the more exciting. What Mr. Boswell might do to me should I write such a story, I could not imagine.

"You are thinking about money," he said of a sudden.

I was not, but it would be next on my list of things to think about.

"Mr. Madalone, senior, has very little money," Boswell said, "but there is an interested benefactor in the case. This benefactor will pay whatever it takes — through the Rocky Mountain Detective Association — to bring the killer to trial."

"I see."

"Two reasons for my coming to you. First, I believe that as a reporter you would help in making the crime public, which could also expose the criminal goings-on of the Kelly Contracting Company. Second, I like your objectivity and the way you go after details."

"Thank you."

"If you were to report that the Association is on Kelly's trail, it could warn him off. I need your list of contacts and could use your help, but I don't want any publicity until the killer is in manacles. I'm prepared to offer you a bargain: you keep my mission a secret and lend me your notebook with the names of those witnesses; in return, you can come along with me to identify Mr. Kane Kelly so that I can arrest him. You can follow the action, so to speak. When I have Kelly secured, you can write the entire story."

"The papers will pay handsomely," I said. "But my funds are too limited just now. I need to turn in copy nearly every day in order to pay my lodging."

"The Association will pay all expenses while we are on the road. Meanwhile, you can probably collect stories along the way and wire them to your newspapers. You are a stringer, are you not?"

"Yes."

Something about Boswell's poise and determination was infectious. I found myself aping his powerful stride as we walked along together, wishing that I had a thick walking stick like his.

"Then I'll do it," I said at last.

"Excellent," he said. "By this time next week, I expect to have my man in handcuffs and you shall have your story."

We returned to my boardinghouse, where Mr. Boswell paid my lodging a month in advance with a check written on the Rocky Mountain Detective Association. I handed him my Fort Steele notebooks.

"Now you have a place to leave your things and no reason to worry about rent money," he said as we parted at the stoop of the boardinghouse. "Much to do today. I suggest we begin by trying to discover the exact whereabouts of our Mr. Kane Kelly. After I deliver your notes to the stenographer, I'll visit the offices of the various railroads and find out where tracks are being laid."

"And I'll search through the morgues of the *Daily Herald* and the *Omaha Republican* for any news stories about track building in the region," I said.

"Excellent," he said again. "Detection is like hunting, Mr. Pierce. We locate our quarry, flush him out, then run him to ground. I'll be in touch with you tomorrow."

Giving me a nod and touching a fingertip to the brim of his bowler hat, the detective strode off. My blood felt hot with excitement. On my way back up to my room, I whispered the famous line that Shakespeare wrote for Henry V.

"The game's afoot: follow your spirit!"

On the following morning N. K. Boswell discovered me at breakfast and accepted a cup of coffee as we exchanged results. It seemed that our two searches had turned up the same information: Kane Kelly had a contract with the Burlington and Missouri Railroad, and his crew was engaged approximately three miles out of a town called Red Oak, Iowa. This explained why the murderer had not been seen in Des Moines or Omaha. Red Oak was forty miles to the south and on a different railroad system. In between was nothing but forty miles of empty country.

"Red Oak presents us with one bit of luck, at least," Mr. Boswell said. "The sheriff of Montgomery County, where Red Oak is located, has cooperated with the Rocky Mountain Detective Association previously, and to his advantage. I wired that selfsame gentleman yesterday afternoon and received his word that he would assist us in the arrest of our man."

"That is good," I said. "Now the problem is how to get there."

"Exactly," Mr. Boswell said. "With tracks under construction, we can't use the Burlington and Missouri. However, I have hired a buggy. We will gather provisions and drive the forty miles to Red Oak."

We made two easy days of it, sometimes being forced into long detours to find creek crossings. The creeks seemed to show up every few miles, mostly sluggish streams meandering through the low hills. We were following a primitive track — two wheel ruts in most places. Each time the track came to a creek, it divided itself with one line of ruts leading along the creek in search of a crossing and the other plunging straight down into the shadowy gully. The river bottoms, or "cuts" as they were called, were densely wooded with abrupt vertical banks and tangles of vines and brush. We tried to avoid them because they harbored a variety of flying insects, besides posing the danger of the team and buggy getting mired or falling off a crumbling creek bank.

I much preferred it when the track led us from hillcrest to hillcrest. From the tops of those Iowa hills, I could see nothing but prairie punctuated far away in all directions by dots of green cottonwoods. The river bottoms could sometimes be seen from a distance as dark lines, but for the most part we bounced along the dirt track and saw nothing but endless expanses of grass. As I remarked to Mr. Boswell, these rolling plains were so vast, they hurt the eyes. Indeed, I felt as though we were two mythical heroes venturing into the unknown, heading into a maze in our quest to bring a devil to judgment.

We arrived in Red Oak late in the afternoon and located the Montgomery County sheriff, a soft-spoken and capable-looking gentleman named Charles Davis. He said he would be ready when we came for him the next morning.

A bachelor homesteader on the outskirts of town was pleased to sell us some grain for the team and allowed us to set up our camp on his property. He said that he had very little occasion to interact with the townspeople, which was to our advantage since Mr. Boswell did not want news of our mission spread abroad. When Mr. Boswell casually asked about the progress of the Burlington and Missouri, our host was only too glad to lead us up a small hill, from which he pointed out the track bed.

"Yonder it goes," he said, pointing toward a barely visible line about two miles distant. "Most folk hereabouts think she's goin' to junction with the Missouri Pacific right outside town. Some hold the opinion that they're goin' to lay track all th' way to the Missouri River and bridge it and go on."

"All the workmen are at the end of track, then?"

"Can't say. There's a deep cut just about there," he said, pointing to the spot, "where some contractor's got men workin' to fix the bank. Embankment, you know. I heard they gotta make 'er wider since she keeps slidin' onto the track."

Mr. Boswell said nothing until he and I were alone again.

"I have a hunch that we'll find our man at that cut," he said.

The morning was bright and clear with no wind. As we drove along, I took out my notebook and asked for more information concerning the Rocky Mountain Detective Association. By coincidence, Sheriff Davis was acquainted with the Association's founder, a gentleman named David J. Cook who had gone to Colorado during the gold rush and then became a government detective there, which led to his being elected sheriff of Arapahoe County. Cook was also a deputy United States marshal.

"We're a private association," Mr. Boswell said to me, "but the sheriff will tell you we are more than that."

"You can see for yourself," said Sheriff Davis. "Just look around! Lawmen like myself are spread awful thin and can't afford many full-time men to help out. We can usually find local deputies. But if a criminal assaults someone and lights a shuck for the open prairie, there's no manpower to track him down. Thanks to the Association, though, I can send a telegram to Denver, or to Laramie City, and they'll contact other marshals and sheriffs. You rob a store or steal a horse in Red Oak and head west, and every lawman on every road and town will hear about it. And if we want you real bad, Association detectives like Mr. Boswell will come track you down!"

"What about a posse?" I asked.

"Don't like using them," Sheriff Davis said. "They're fine for making a search, say, if a child goes missing on the prairie. But a posse is mostly citizens with jobs and shops to look after, so they're always anxious to get back. Some of them tend to be trigger-happy. And bein' your pioneer stock, they're mostly too damn independent to take orders. No, I almost never use a posse in a criminal matter."

In due course we arrived at the railroad tracks. Now the question was, in which direction would we find the construction gang? Eastward the terrain looked to be flat as a floor, nothing but the endless ocean of grass with the long, long stretch of steel rails vanishing into a shimmering mirage at the horizon. Westward those same rails disappeared into a region of rising and falling hills. We reasoned that if the rails passed through a "cut," it would be in that direction. And we were correct: we soon spotted a gang of workmen hacking away at the side of the tracks where the railroad bed had been routed through a low hill.

"We'll drive on past," Mr. Boswell said. "As if we are going somewhere else. Keep a sharp eye on the gang, however, and see whether you can spot anyone resembling Mr. Kelly."

I looked at the workers as we drove by, nodding to one or two of them. They silently watched us in return.

"No Kelly," I said when we were clear of the gang.

"We'll go on a ways," Mr. Boswell said.

We had driven almost a mile farther up the tracks when we spotted a lone figure, a man standing on the other side of another railroad cut.

Mr. Boswell stopped the buggy and got out to assess the situation. The embankment was steep, but not overly so. It would be possible to scramble up the opposite side. Mr. Boswell returned to our buggy. As he did so, the man on the other side of the cut walked nearer the edge to get a better look at us.

"What do you think?" Mr. Boswell asked me. "Is that our man Kelly?"

"I'm certain of it," I said. "As soon as he began to walk toward us, I recognized his swagger, the way he swings his arms as if angry. Yes, that's him all right."

"Then we will have him," said Mr. Boswell.

Sheriff Davis stepped down from the buggy. As he reached the ground and joined Mr. Boswell, the man on the other side of the cut turned abruptly and began to walk away from us. There was no mistaking that stride and the indignant swinging of the arms. It was Kane Kelly, the murderer of

Charlie Madalone. I don't think he knew who we were, but he would take no chances talking to strangers.

Mr. Boswell shouted for him to stop.

"Kelly! Kane Kelly, stop there! Come back here! We want a word with you!"

Kelly, however, saw no reason to get into conversation with three men he did not know. He kept walking, evidently intent on reaching a wagon and team parked a half mile away.

"Kane Kelly!" the detective shouted again. "This is Sheriff Davis! I am a private detective and we are asking you to talk to us! Come back!"

Kelly kept walking.

Mr. Boswell and Sheriff Davis hesitated no longer, but slid down the railroad embankment, crossed the rail bed and crawled up the other side. I took a moment to secure the lines lest the team decide to wander off and then I, too, slid down the embankment and up the opposite side. I ran until I had caught up with Sheriff Davis and Mr. Boswell. They were walking quickly and continued to shout for Kelly to stop.

Mr. Boswell yelled the final warning.

"Kelly! You are wanted for murder! Stop right now! Stop or I will shoot you down!"

Kelly paid no attention, however. He kept

on going, and it was evident he would reach the wagon before we could reach him.

Detective Boswell had had enough of this footrace. He carried two pistols, one at his hip and the other in a shoulder holster. He drew out the latter, cocked it, knelt down on the ground and steadied the weapon on his knee. There was the sound of the shot and I saw Kelly throw up his hands and stop in his tracks. Then he turned and seemed about to topple over.

"My God!" Kelly screamed. "Stop! Stop firing! You have wounded me! I surrender! Don't shoot me again!"

When we got to him, Kelly was lying on the ground. The pistol ball had caught him in the small of the back, but it appeared to have missed his spine. A bloodstained rip in the front of his waistcoat indicated that it had exited his body somewhere near his navel. Miraculously, there was little blood and he did not seem seriously disabled. Nevertheless, as Sheriff Davis and Mr. Boswell pulled him to his feet and started walking him back to our buggy, Kelly kept up a string of oaths and complaints.

"You've killed me!" he cried. "Murdered! In cold blood, you bastard! You have shot me in the back like a coward and you shall pay! This is not a legitimate arrest, as you have killed me by shooting me in the back! Let me lie down here and die! Send for some men to help me! Oh! Killers! I'm in the hands of killers! Oh, who will help me!"

Sheriff Davis relieved Kelly of the pistol he was carrying, and he and Mr. Boswell assisted Kelly in stumbling along. The prisoner kept up his harangue and wailing. While they were skidding him down the side of the embankment and prodding him to climb up the other side, I stepped off the distance between where Mr. Boswell had fired and where Kelly had fallen. It seemed incredible to me, so I counted my strides back to the same spot again. I had not been mistaken. With a revolver, Mr. Boswell had hit his target at approximately two hundred yards.

CHAPTER 3

The detective and sheriff had their man, but now a new danger presented itself. A mean-looking bunch of the contractor's men was hurrying toward us. One of them had probably heard the shot and had seen Kelly being dragged back to the buggy. Here came the entire gang to find out what was going on, carrying shovels and pry bars. Those who didn't have tools were carrying rocks and sticks. The mob was being led by a particularly disagreeable-looking fellow. He was in his undershirt with bright yellow braces over it and his battered hat was tilted over one eye.

"This should be interesting," the sheriff whispered to me. "Watch!"

Mr. Boswell was not a man to stand and wait while trouble approached. Leaving us standing with Kelly, he boldly advanced toward the gang without hesitation. His stride was firm, presenting the picture of a man walking up to seize the reins of a runaway horse. Halfway to them he came to a stop and raised his hand in the air, two fingers extended. Standing between them and the buggy, the confidence and assertiveness of his manner halted the men in their tracks. Only one man kept coming, the scowling fellow in the plug hat and dirty undershirt. He moved forward like a barroom bully looking for a fistfight. But then he, too, stopped in the face of Mr. Boswell's calm gaze.

"That is my brother you have there!" plug hat said. "What do you think you are up to?"

"If this is your brother," said Mr. Boswell, "then I know who *you* are, Sligo Kelly. There is a price on your head for that little matter of assault in Kansas City, and the Association will be glad to know your whereabouts. After I dispose of Kane, I may return with papers and place you under arrest as well, so be warned."

"What's wrong with my brother?" Sligo snarled. "He looks like he's hurt! Have you beaten him? Y'got no right t' be holding him like that."

"He resisted arrest and I shot him," Mr. Boswell calmly replied. "We will take him to a doctor and then to jail to await trial. I am an Association detective, duly deputized. I carry a warrant for Kane Kelly for the murder of Charlie Madalone. This other gentleman you know, I'm sure. Sheriff Davis?"

"That murder was over two years ago!" Sligo Kelly said.

"If it were two *score* years ago, we would still be after the culprit if we wanted him. The Association does not quit the chase, as you will soon discover if you try to flee this region."

"You can't take Kane away," Sligo said.

"We'll see about that, won't we?" Mr. Boswell said. "We came for him, and we will take him with us. Keep your distance and tell your men to do the same."

With that he turned on his heel and walked back to us. He ordered Kelly into the buggy, but the wounded man cried and complained that he could not do it because of the pain.

"Very well," Mr. Boswell said, keeping his eye on Sligo Kelly's bunch. "Sheriff Davis, if Mr. Kelly does not climb into that buggy immediately, I want you to shoot him down. He is a crawling, cowardly murderer. I have a warrant for him, and I will waste no more time executing it."

Upon hearing this, Kelly suddenly recovered the use of his legs and arms and was soon seated in the buggy. Mr. Boswell asked me to step up next and requested that I take the lines and drive the team. He covered the crowd with his pistols until Sheriff Davis was in, then he himself got in and we drove off. The crowd yelled and threatened and swore at us. A few rocks were thrown, but with Mr. Boswell's pistols trained upon the gang from the rear seat, the men did not dare to follow.

Now the full seriousness of the matter had time to sink in. There were only the two officers, a reporter and a prisoner. Behind us a brute of a man and a mob of his hunkies were plotting how best to follow us, subdue us and free Kane Kelly. The town of Red Oak was not far away, but beyond Red Oak, we had forty miles of open country to cross. We were conveying a wounded man, the extent of his injury still unknown. It would be necessary to pause at Red Oak, where our reception was by no means certain, and hope that medical assistance would be available there. At that point Sheriff Davis might elect to leave us, and Mr. Boswell and I would attempt the long drive north to the railroad that could carry us to Laramie City. Anywhere along that route, and indeed anywhere along the railroad, should we make it that far, Sligo Kelly and his toughs could ambush us.

"So, Mr. Pierce," Mr. Boswell said as he settled into the seat and began to reload the spent chamber of his revolver, "do you think you'll have enough material for your story?"

"More than enough, I fear!"

"There is nothing more I can do for this man," said the physician in Red Oak. "Very little blood, considering the ball passed through his abdomen. I'll give you extra wrappings so you can change them each day."

"Will he survive the trip to Pacific Junction, do you think?" asked Mr. Boswell.

"Frankly, Detective, I don't know. Seeing as how he's not dead already, my guess is that he will heal. A buggy trip might dislodge some vital organ, but I very much doubt it. I've seen hunters and soldiers recover completely from worse belly wounds than his."

"Then we will go," Mr. Boswell said. "A westbound train is due to arrive at Pacific Junction in two days' time. I intend to meet it."

He asked for paper and a pen and wrote down the address of the Rocky Mountain Detective Association.

"If you will send your bill to this office," he said, "payment will be arranged."

Detective Boswell went to the telegraph office to send wires reporting our progress and alerting a Council Bluffs colleague concerning our planned arrival. Sheriff Davis and I got Kelly back into the buggy and drove to the livery to grain and water the horses, after which we made a brief visit to the sheriff's house. For a moment I was afraid when he left me alone with the prisoner and went inside for a few necessaries. I stood up in the buggy, forced myself to turn and look at Kelly, and my fear vanished. I drew myself to my full height and glared down on the cringing criminal, almost daring him to look me in the eye. In that single minute, I believe, I began to fully appreciate how it would feel to be a Boswell or a Davis, confronting evil in the line of duty. It must be a very satisfying feeling, indeed. Made the blood rush and the pulse beat stronger.

Sheriff Davis returned with his small carpet bag. We picked up Detective Boswell, and the four of us were off again and making quick time. The broad road north passed a few farmsteads, became a single track, passed a couple of shacks and became a faint trail that wound along the grassy heights and curved down into the shaded creek bottoms. Kane Kelly complained loudly for the first few miles before slumping into silence. Sheriff Davis, who had declared in Red Oak that he would not be left behind to miss this great venture, drove the team and chatted about the Iowa landscape as if we were headed out for a picnic. Meanwhile, Detective Boswell meticulously checked the loads of his two revolvers.

"Hand me your pistols," he said to Davis. "I'll check them while you drive."

With each mile we covered, we became more at ease; it appeared that the Kelly mob was not following us.

"We'll drive on through the night," Mr. Boswell decided. "There will be a fair moon and we should not lose our way. The key thing is to meet that train at Pacific Junction."

We made steady progress as the evening shadows grew longer and darker. Mr. Boswell began to relax his rearward vigil. The prisoner had ceased complaining about his wound, his unfair treatment and his general situation and even seemed to doze off from time to time. A mile or two beyond the halfway point of our trip, we made a stop at a crude farm, a homestead whose occupants knew Sheriff Davis. They were pleased to sell us some bread and jerked meat and allowed us to water the team. They urged us to stay the night. Mr. Boswell, however, repeated that we were hurrying to meet the weekly train at Pacific Junction. And within a half hour we were back on the road again.

We drove along in silence. I noticed that Detective Boswell seemed very thoughtful all of a sudden, as if he were lost in a reverie of some sort. After many minutes he told us what was worrying him.

"Gentlemen," he said, meaning myself and Sheriff Davis, "I have made a greenhorn's error. At the doctor's office in Red Oak and again at the cabin back there, I let it be known that we are heading for Pacific Junction and that the timing of our arrival is critical. If Mr. Kelly's brother and his confederates hear of it, and if they are bright enough to add two and two, they will figure out our route and will know that any delay would be greatly to their advantage. This is the only wagon road to Pacific Junction, and we must stay on it if we are to catch the train in time. But a group of men on horseback could cut across country and be there before us."

"Will they set up an ambush?" I asked.

"That, or they'll overtake us. And try to

stop us. Either way, I apologize to you gentlemen for my mistake."

Although night was fast approaching, we still had plenty of light for traveling. We had arrived in an expanse of river bottom land where the track made its way through flat, lush meadows and in and out of shady copses of cottonwood and elm. Under ordinary circumstances it would have been an ideal place for an evening buggy ride, a kind of idyllic spot among the hills. The peacefulness of the place, however, was suddenly blasted.

"Someone coming!" the sheriff announced.

I turned to look back. We were being overtaken by a mounted party, and there was little doubt but that it was Kelly's brother and a gang of assailants. The group looked to consist of nearly twenty men, mounted on a variety of mules and plugs. I could see a wagon following them with several men in it, bringing up the rear of their posse. The group was strung out for a hundred yards but were certain to bunch up as soon as they realized we had seen them.

"I see we are coming to another creek up ahead," said Detective Boswell. "Or else that line of trees indicates a swale beside the track. Do you recognize where we are, Sheriff?"

"Yes," said Sheriff Davis. "They call it Turtle Creek. The road meets the stream down among those trees, just there. There's a good place to ford, wide and with good footing. Then it goes up the hill on the opposite side, and after that we'll be out on the open flats again."

"Then by all means let's whip up the team and get across the stream. If it's a good wide ford as you said, I think we'll halt on the other side and see what these rogues want."

Sheriff Davis put the team into a trot, and in less time than it takes to tell, we had splashed across the stream and stopped in the deep shadows of the trees on the opposite bank. Given our situation, it was the best place to be. I had to admire Mr. Boswell's tactic. We were on a shaded slope with the light behind us. The ford made a flat, open stretch of water that mirrored the sky. The men coming up the road behind us would have a hard time seeing us in the shadows, whereas they would make very clear targets the moment they rode out into the stream.

"Now, Mr. Pierce," said Mr. Boswell. "You are a noncombatant in this issue. I would appreciate it if you would get down and hold the team for us. Should things become too hot, I suggest that you sprint for the cover of those trees downstream and try to return to the farm we stopped at earlier."

"I understand," I said.

"And Sheriff," Mr. Boswell continued, "if you would just put your pistol to Kelly's ear now. And blow the top of his head off if he makes any wrong move, or if his friends do. The three of us are going to Pacific Junction together or we are going to hell together."

The tone of his voice must have chilled Kane Kelly's spine. It would have frightened me had I not seen Mr. Boswell wink and nudge the sheriff as he said it.

"Well, Mr. Kane Kelly," Mr. Boswell said. "Here they come. I see that your brother has armed some of his ruffians with pistols, pitchforks and clubs. Quite a formidable farewell party for you. I hope they have brought a shovel or two. They might have to dig you a grave."

"You wouldn't shoot me in cold blood!" Kelly wailed.

"Let me be very clear, Kelly," the detective said. "I am not a law officer and therefore not bound by legalities. I have been hired to see to the punishment of the man who murdered Charlie Madalone. That man is you, and your execution might as well take place right here. Either your brother will retreat and we will drive on, or you will die here. And don't deceive yourself into thinking he might rescue you by force. As you can see, we have the advantage of a clear field of fire. We have no fewer than six loaded revolvers among us. If your brother persists and will not turn back, we will give them the best we have in the shop. You, of course, will no longer be alive to see the outcome."

Kane Kelly trembled and wailed.

"What sort of way is this to treat me?" he bawled. "I've been wounded, man! You have shot me and trussed me up. You've bounced me along this road when you knew I was bleeding inside! I don't deserve this. It's brutal, that's what it is! Untie me, just untie me and let me go to my brother. He will take me to a doctor. You men can ride away and no harm done. I beg you, in the name of God, let me go!"

His words fell on deaf ears. With a sneer of disdain, Detective Boswell repeated his instructions to Sheriff Davis.

"If they begin shooting," he said, "or if Kelly tries to run for it, please put a bullet through his head."

He stepped from the buggy and walked to

the water's edge to confront the mob.

He looked very alone. I stood in front of the team holding them by their headstalls and watched the drama as it unfolded.

The ugly Irishman in the plug hat was nowhere in sight. He had been replaced, apparently, the new leader of the bunch being a lean, evil-looking man in a wide brimmed hat and dark coat.

"That ugly piece of work is Clifton, the other Kelly brother," Sheriff Davis told me. "My guess is that Sligo did not want to take the risk of being arrested. Clifton is less likely to be intimidated by Boswell. Too bad he is in the shadows so you can't see his nasty face. If you want to know what he looks like, imagine the face of a fox biting down on a sour persimmon."

Clifton Kelly and three others rode into the stream and paused halfway across.

"Now, then," Detective Boswell called to them. "What is it you want?"

"My brother, of course! We want Kane, and this time we mean to take him!"

"Oh, you do? Well, if that is all there is to it, then you must come across and get him."

Kane Kelly's nerve had completely left him by this point. He turned in the buggy as far as his bound hands would permit, moving gingerly so as not to jostle the

66

revolver whose muzzle was pressed to his ear. In his fancy, he could probably hear the hammer falling already. In that whining tone we had grown so used to, he called out to his "rescuers."

"Is that you, Cliff? For God's sake! Don't make a move! I've got a gun to my head and they'll kill me if you make a move!"

His brother was not the only man who heard this cowardly bawling. It reached the ears of the rabble with clubs and pitchforks on the other side of the stream. They began murmuring among themselves.

"Mr. Kelly," said Detective Boswell, addressing Clifton. "No doubt you are new to this sort of situation. I hope you see that you cannot predict the outcome. The kindly thing, then, is for me to explain. You see, I have played out this same little drama several times. And Sheriff Davis has experience as well. You are an illegal mob intending to do an illegal act. We are lawmen legally conducting a prisoner to trial. Understand?"

There was no reply. The mob had stopped muttering. Mr. Boswell had their attention.

"You have exactly two options here and no more," he continued. "You can turn and ride back down the trail and enjoy an early breakfast and a nice sunrise. Or you can continue across this stream and attempt to free your murdering coward of a brother. But I repeat, we are a private detective and an officer of the law, taking a prisoner to a fair trial. Therefore, any attack upon us will be treated as interference with the law."

Clifton Kelly snorted at this. But he remained where he was.

"We are too many for you!" Clifton said.

"Cliff!" It was Kane Kelly calling from the buggy. "Cliff! Don't try it or we'll both be dead! Don't try!"

Detective Boswell let Kane have his say and then addressed Clifton again.

"Is it still not clear to you?" he said. "If your little army begins to attack us, the whole thing changes. Sheriff Davis and I will become quite busy at that point. We would not want Kane to seize a gun and begin shooting from the buggy, so Davis will immediately put the first ball through Kane's skull, and he will no longer pose a threat to us.

"At nearly the same instant I will draw and shoot the four of you from the saddle. If you know my reputation for marksmanship, you know that I can do it. I intend to shoot any man who displays a firearm. The sheriff will also open fire, and between us we will kill several of your confederates before they break and run. Of course they will leave you and your lieutenants bleeding in the stream. I'm afraid your bodies will have to remain there since we have no time for burials."

"I'm not afraid of you," Clifton Kelly said.

But his assertion lacked conviction. I think it had finally sunk in that he had never shot at a human being, while the detective who confronted him had probably killed dozens.

"Just so we are clear," Mr. Boswell finished. "You are the leader, so you will be my first target. And as your brother will attest, I hit what I aim at."

Kane Kelly called out from the buggy. "Cliff, for God's sake! He means to kill me! Call off the men! I need a doctor or else I'll die out here in this wilderness. Please, Cliff! Don't let anyone start shooting, or this sheriff will kill me like a stray dog. This ain't the time to start anything! Best let them get me to a doctor! Cry off! Cry off!"

"You haven't heard the end of this," Clifton yelled at the detective. "Not by a long chalk! Here's my bargain: if you promise to see that my brother is cared for, we will retreat and bother you no more today. But if he dies, you look out."

"Until he dies," Mr. Boswell said coolly, "we will look to our revolvers. And now we will be going."

The detective turned his back upon the hoodlums and returned to the buggy. The mob, true to Kelly's promise, turned away and rode back into the darkening shadows. As the last man vanished into the gloom, I drew a deep breath as if I had not been breathing for an hour. And I had been holding the team's headstall so firmly that my fingers were painfully cramped.

"Not much of a gang," said Mr. Boswell as he climbed into the buggy. "Most of them working men with families back home, I assume. I would hazard a guess that most of them were wondering what they were doing here in the first place, following that rat-faced individual into a gunfight."

That was the last we saw of the Kelly rescue mob during the remainder of our drive; Sheriff Davis estimated that we would reach Pacific Junction in plenty of time to meet the weekly westbound train. I felt proud to be in the company of these two men. Although I had no part in the confrontation with Kelly's mob, I felt somehow bolder and stronger than I had ever felt in my life.

CHAPTER 4

The slow coming of the morning light revealed to the eye an endless, monotonous repetition of low hills and shadowed creek beds. Despite the swaying and bouncing of the buggy, I was half asleep, nodding and dreaming that we were ancient travelers in some kind of myth, doomed to wander forever in this ocean of grass. Now and then a jolt would bring a moan from the prisoner; in the dreams of my half sleep, these seemed to be like the groans of spirits trapped in the desolate swales around us. It was Sheriff Davis's exclamation that roused me from my uneasy sleep.

"There it is!"

My eyes opened reluctantly and blinked without comprehension. I was looking all around like a student who had been caught napping during lessons, and at first I saw nothing but empty prairie. Then I did see it, where the sheriff was pointing: a slender column of smoke rising into the air just beyond the horizon. My first thought was that it must be coming from the train we expected to meet, but as the sleep left my head and I came back to full consciousness I realized it was not moving. Chimney smoke. It meant there must be a house or a town.

"There it is," the sheriff repeated. "That has to be Pacific Junction over that hill, and none too soon to suit me. A long night, wasn't it, boys? Look there! A rider coming!"

Detective Boswell drew one of his revolvers and checked the caps.

The rider was coming straight toward us, moving fast, riding straight and tall in the saddle with the easy poise of the western horseman. He rode right at us without hesitation until he came abreast of our team and reined up. He was a young man; the broad Stetson, the bandanna knotted around his neck, the tall boots and Spanish spurs showed us that he was a cowboy, or had been one not too long ago. I could see only one detail out of place, which was that he wore two revolvers, whereas most range cowboys only carried one. A working cowhand rarely if ever needed to use one gun, let alone two. Most of them couldn't afford two guns and had no use for a second one. But, as I had learned from Detective Boswell, a law officer sometimes needed a second weapon. A cowboy shooting a rattler or putting an animal out of pain could take time to clear a jammed cylinder or reload a bad charge; a lawman in a gunfight did not have that luxury and needed another weapon to hand instantly.

Detective Boswell holstered his weapon and smiled broadly.

"Hayward Campbell, or else I'm a liar!" Mr. Boswell said cheerily.

"Aye, the same!" said the rider. His accent betrayed a Scottish background, and none too far distant either. "It's good to see you, Mr. Boswell!"

"Out for a morning ride?" Mr. Boswell smiled. "Taking some exercise?"

"Oh, aye. I dearly love to be up before breakfast and ride out to see what's changed with these blasted prairies overnight."

"Hayward, I'd like you to meet these men. Himself handling the lines is Sheriff Davis of Red Oak. You've heard of him. Back here beside me is our chronicler, Mr. Phillip Pierce, of the *Omaha Daily Herald*. And the gent lying on the floorboards is my prisoner, Kane Kelly."

"And he slaughtered that young lad at

Fort Steele," the Scots cowboy added.

"Correct. We're hoping to catch the weekly train to Laramie City. Gentlemen, this Celtic *caballero* is Deputy Marshal Hayward Campbell, one of the youngest and most enthusiastic members of the Rocky Mountain Detective Association. He came west to become a cowboy and found that he was more adept at catching men than steers or mustangs."

It turned out that Mr. Campbell had known we were coming and rode out in order to intercept us and give us a warning. From him we learned that, although Clifton Kelly and his mob had been true to their word and left us unmolested during the night, they had hurried to Pacific Junction by a more direct route than the buggy road and were there ahead of us.

"I was waiting in Pacific Junction to meet that same train, as it turned out," Campbell said. "I am after a man rumored to be working at Plattesmouth on the other side of the Missouri. As soon as I heard Clifton's crew blathering on about wanting to stop 'that damn Boswell' from putting Kelly on that train, I knew you were coming and figured I needed to get to you before they did. He's gathered a couple dozen rogues to block you."

"And what's the layout?" the detective asked.

"There's the usual. The town's just a line of one street with buildings either side. Alley behind. The rail station platform is a large one, built over a swampy bog. It connects the hotel with the rails. That's where they'll lay for you, on that platform. Right now some are sleeping on the platform. Or else hunting up breakfast or a drink. I wandered among 'em a bit. The most of them are only there because they work for the contractor, or hope to. Couldn't care less about Kelly. They're as smelly a gatherin' of unredeemed bastards as I've ever seen."

"Suggestions?"

"Mr. Boswell, your train is due to pull into the station pretty soon. We've got an hour, maybe two. If I were you, I would drive off the road right here and now. I'd circle around that last hill. From there I think we can make it to the livery unnoticed. From the livery it's a few steps across the corner to the hotel. Where we can wait for the train."

"We?" the sheriff said.

"Oh, aye! I'm with you, if you'll have me. I knew young Charlie Madalone, you see. And I'm an officer of the law. Damned if

I'll see a mob set Charlie's murderer free again. Even if that were not the case, I like what the Association does. I believe in it. My guns are always in the service of the Association. Y'may already have learned, Sheriff, that Detective Boswell is one of the best of our number. It'd be an honor to stand with him. Not that this bunch of cowards will give much trouble. Mostly they're on the Kelly payroll and afraid to look disloyal to the company. They've no love for the Kelly brothers themselves. Most of them are not even armed, save for a few knives and an ax handle or two."

Somehow this did not sound comforting to me, but the detective seemed unconcerned.

"Let's make for that hotel, then," he said. "Lead on."

Crossing those miles of open prairie, I compared our little group to the soldiers in *Henry V,* the king's "band of brothers," slight in number but strong in will and determination. In the frontier's vastness, a man had but two choices: to stand tall and persevere in the face of storm and heat, or go to ground like an animal. Now that we were huddled in a dark, dusty corner of the Pacific Junction hotel I felt more like Hamlet, surrounded by enemies, victim of my own uncertainties. Why was I in this predicament? What manner of pride or self-deception had brought me here? I had no answers. I was aware, however, of a feeling that in the company of these three brave men, these supremely confident men, there was nowhere I would rather be.

My somber reflections were broken by the welcome sound of a train whistle. Mr. Boswell ventured to draw the window curtain aside just far enough to peer out.

"Here she comes," he whispered. "She'll stop long enough to take on water and wood. Mr. Pierce, come here."

I stepped over to where he was standing.

"Do you have train fare?"

"I still have my rail pass from the Cheyenne *Leader,*" I explained. "It will guarantee my passage."

"Very good. Do you wish to continue with us?"

I looked into his deep, cool eyes. I was honored by the question.

"Yes."

He looked out the window again and studied the situation.

"I make it about thirty men crowded onto that platform," the detective said. "They should give us no trouble. However, the train itself could be a problem. I was expecting a string of passenger cars, but all I can see from here is freight cars."

He looked again.

"Yes, it's a freight with no passenger cars. We shall have to improvise. The car at the end, the one just before the caboose, seems to be empty. Its doors are open. We can use it."

"Whatever you think best, Detective," I said. "What do you want me to do?"

"Mr. Pierce, I want you to leave through the back door, the way we came in. As unobtrusively as possible, make your way around the building and move toward the front of the train. You should be able to take advantage of the steam and noise coming from the engine. It will hide your movements from that crowd on the dock. You will sneak around the front of the engine to the opposite side. But act casually and if someone does see you, you are only a traveler killing time by looking at the locomotive and cars. From the other side of the engine you can make your way to that rear car, where we will meet you."

"I understand," I said.

"One thing further. The conductor might be near the engine, helping with the wood or water, or perhaps he will be inspecting wheels on the cars. If you encounter him, please let him know what we are doing."

My pulse was racing. Once more I was going to witness the machinations of Detective Boswell's keen mind and grasp of tactics. Walking through the dimly lit room toward the door, I felt feverish with intense excitement. I was champing at the bit for the moment when I could write this adventure down in my notebook. I wasn't even thinking of a story for the newspapers. I only wanted to try and capture it all in writing.

I carefully opened the rear door of the hotel building and, as naturally as I could with my heart pounding and palms sweating, I sidled along the building to the corner. From there on I would be in the open until I made it to the engine. It took all of my self-control to walk nonchalantly and slowly, as if I were just out for a stroll and was curious about the locomotive. My steps took me around the edge of that evil-smelling lagoon between hotel and tracks. As I neared the engine, I was glad to see it was puffing clouds of steam from somewhere beneath its iron belly. With those steam clouds between me and the crowd on the platform, I was able to cross the tracks unobserved. I did see the conductor, but he was atop the tender helping the fireman hold the water spout. Neither man took any notice of me.

Still walking as casually as possible, I went down along the string of cars until I came to the last one just ahead of the caboose. It was empty except for a few crates and bales. I climbed in through the open doorway and crossed to the opposite side. Safely hidden in the shadows behind the heavy door, I had a clear view of the hotel and the freight platform built over the muddy slough. The door would offer protection from any stray pistol balls that might happen to come my way, a detail I found rather comforting, despite my newfound self-confidence. Once or twice during my adventure I had imagined a headline in the *Herald* that would read "Detective Association Gets Its Man." It would hardly do if that headline should turn out to say "*Herald* Reporter Shot in Line of Duty."

The mob on the platform looked disorganized and unmotivated but still presented a formidable appearance. Most of the men were unarmed, being woodcutters, freighters and railroad laborers. Clifton Kelly was moving among them, shouting and slapping men on the shoulders as he made his way toward the stock pen. He was waving a revolver and loudly swearing to his brother's innocence — overlooking the possibility that several men in that same crowd might have actually witnessed the murder — and crying about "unlawful arrest" and "no jurisdiction" and other such rubbish. The toughs closest to him would respond by raising fists in the air and calling out oaths; however, as soon as he moved on to another clot of thugs, the first bunch would fall silent. It was all too obvious that they were in it because Kelly, Inc., paid their wages. Clifton had probably told them that the arrest and conviction of Kane Kelly would mean the end of their employment. This argument, however, must have been transparent to at least half of them, however dull they were. In those days along the railroad, an able workman could find a job virtually anywhere. Labor was scarce and the various railroads were competing at a furious pace to lay tracks.

"All you gotta do t'get a job is just pick up a shovel or a pick and tell the foreman to write your name down on the pay sheet," one laborer had told me in Fort Steele.

There was a loud creaking and clatter of chains from the front of the train as the big metal spout was swung away and hoisted back upright at the water tower. It meant that the water tender was now full and the train would be pulling out in a matter of minutes. I leaned out to look and saw the hotel door opening. I expected to see my colleagues slipping quietly into the platform gang, trying to be as unobtrusive as possible. Instead, Detective Boswell's big voice boomed out loud and clear.

"Now is our time, boys!"

The mob turned to see where the voice had come from. They had been told that the lawman and his prisoner would be arriving by buggy from the other direction. They were not certain who this new arrival might be. They looked to Clifton Kelly for orders, but he was over by the corral somewhere. Confusion spread.

My first thought was that Detective Boswell's strategy must have taken the prisoner's brother by complete surprise. But where was he? Even with my higher vantage point in the freight car I could not see him at first. He was nowhere near the hotel doorway. When I finally located the wide dark hat, it seemed to be rising up out of the crowd.

Expecting to see our buggy coming into the station from the other direction, Clifton Kelly was climbing up onto a corner of the stock pen near the engine. He stood there balancing on the top rails. The most fervent of his followers clustered around him, while the less bold ones hung back and stayed closer to the hotel. The men near the hotel had been confused and agitated by the exclamation "Now is our time!" coming from behind them and by the sudden appearance of the sheriff and the deputy marshal calmly walking out of the doorway, each officer showing a pair of cocked revolvers. Prisoner Kelly walked behind the two lawmen. His hands were securely bound and tethered by a short cord to the belt of Mr. Boswell, who brought up the rear with both of his revolvers at the ready.

"It's Kane Kelly!"

The word spread from man to man.

"Tell them, Kane Kelly!" Mr. Boswell said in his loud and commanding voice. "Tell your men to open up and let us through! From this point on, I have nothing to lose by shooting you."

"Oh, make way, boys!" Kelly wailed. "He keeps threatening to kill me! Out of the way!"

In contrast to Mr. Boswell's firm, clear voice, Kelly's sounded more like that of a child who had fallen and skinned a knee.

"Please make way!" he yowled. "This man means to shoot me down if you do not let us through! For the love of God, spread out! Oh, make way! Make way!"

The mob divided like the Red Sea in the story of Moses. The bullies standing nearest the cocked pistols of the officers pushed backward frantically, shoving into their own comrades. Oaths and mutterings rose from the group, especially from those who were farther removed from the field of fire. Then there was a general heaving and milling of the bunch on the platform. Before the wave of surprise and confusion could reach the rear of the mob, the sheriff and deputy marshal had reached the freight car.

"Close that other door!" Deputy Campbell exclaimed, and I jumped to do it.

Campbell and Sheriff Davis leapt up into the car and turned to haul the prisoner up. As Detective Boswell turned his back to the crowd in order to mount the car someone hurled a chunk of firewood and caught him between the shoulders. The detective stumbled a little, then turned. Aiming both his revolvers over the heads of the mob he cut loose with two shots simultaneously.

"And in an instant," as the poet Robert Burns wrote, the swarm of bully boys had turned into a rout, with those near the tracks shoving and climbing the ones behind them in their panic to get away. The ones at the rear were running for their lives; a dozen had fallen off the platform into the mucky water, and several dashed into the hotel where they slammed the door against their own comrades. In the far distance beyond the lagoon a few more men were running across a field of wheat. You may think this showed an excess of cowardice; however, many of those men had seen military action firsthand and knew all too well what it would mean to face six repeating pistols firing into their mass.

Detective Boswell and Sheriff Davis stood together in the car's doorway laughing merrily at the sight. One rogue picked up another piece of firewood, intending to stand his ground, but when the sheriff leveled a revolver at him, he dropped it and ran to bang on the hotel door for admission.

During this melee Clifton Kelly had remained balanced atop his fence corner, screaming at his remaining followers to "get 'em, get 'em!"

And then Clifton made his mistake.

He drew out a pistol and fired it at us.

The booming report of his gun froze the remnants of the mob. Then all heads turned toward the puff of gun smoke and the man standing atop the corral rails.

"Now he's done it," said Detective Boswell. "I was hoping he would."

The detective took his stance in the doorway of the boxcar and calmly took aim. His pistol ball struck Clifton Kelly in the thigh, and with a scream and an oath the mob leader went crashing down into the muck and manure of the stock pen. The sight of Mr. Boswell in the doorway with his revolver was sufficient to immobilize most of the crowd, although it did not discourage four or five of Kelly's bunch who now decided to make a rush at us.

Oddly enough, I was not afraid. I suppose it was due to the fact that the drama I was witnessing had grabbed my interest so completely that all personal thoughts were banished from my mind. I even smiled: Deputy Campbell was laughing and enjoying himself as he shoved one man down between the tracks and the platform, punched another in the nose and used the barrel of his revolver to render a third one unconscious. The dangerous violence seemed to be a bit of a game or some kind of recreation for him. The sheriff kicked another thug away from the boxcar, and as the train began to move away, I saw two would-be assailants running alongside the caboose behind us, cursing us and waving their fists in the empty air.

My lack of fear had taken me by surprise. As I saw the sheriff and the deputy clap one another on the shoulder and shake hands, grinning broadly, I thought I understood. The men on that platform were violent, disorganized, afraid *not* to act; we few were calm and determined, and in that fact lay all the difference.

After our exciting getaway, the train ride to Council Bluffs was so peaceful as to seem almost idyllic. We lounged against sacks of grain and bales of wool and enjoyed the scenery. Deputy Campbell spun out some stories of his experiences in the West, and his rolling Scots accent had a lyrical quality to it. Detective Boswell stood near the opening, smoking his pipe. We left the doors open, allowing the breeze to flow through the car. Perhaps I should say that *some* of us were enjoying the breeze from the open doors, *some* of us liked watching the landscape rushing past us at forty miles per hour.

Mr. Kane Kelly was not enjoying himself at all. He was provided with sacks of grain by way of cushioning his body against the bumping of the car, but he could only lie there with his legs drawn up to his chest, whimpering and groaning. Fresh blood began to stain his shirt in the area of his wound, and he seemed to be getting quite pale in the face. By the time we arrived in Council Bluffs, Kane Kelly's physical condition looked serious.

"The prisoner needs medical attention," said Detective Boswell as we prepared to disembark from the freight car. "Without it, I'm afraid he might not survive the rest of the journey to Laramie City. Dead or alive doesn't matter much to me, but I suppose I have an obligation to try to bring him to trial. Alive."

I volunteered to find a physician and bring him to the jail where Mr. Boswell was to arrange temporary lodging for Mr. Kelly. Like the previous doctor, this one was surprised that the pistol ball had passed through Kelly's lower body without hitting a vital organ — otherwise the man would be dead by now.

"No blood in your urine?" he said. "Well, I don't understand how, but that bullet appears to have gone clear through you without rupturing your plumbing. It's lucky you're alive."

He prescribed two weeks of rest, after which Kelly would be fit to travel. In order to be certain there were no complications, he agreed to attend Kelly every other day during our stay in Council Bluffs.

When the doctor had left and the jail cell clicked shut on Kane Kelly, Detective Boswell turned to his little posse with a smile of satisfaction.

"Gentlemen," he said, "I cannot tell you how much I have enjoyed your company and your assistance. Rest assured I will be writing commendations to your superiors. Meanwhile, I have made out these chits — one for each of you — and if you will fill in your expenses and post these to the office of the Rocky Mountain Detective Association, your compensation will be forthcoming. Mr. Pierce, you may do me just one more service. I suspect you are eager to cross over the river to Omaha in order to publish your story. If you could omit the information that Kelly and I will be stopping here in Council Bluffs for two weeks . . ."

"I understand," I said. "You need not worry about my news story, Detective! I will end with our thrilling escape from the crowd of ruffians at Pacific Junction and say that *I* reached Omaha without any further excitement. Which is the truth."

"Unless your ferry sinks in the Missouri and you don't *reach* Omaha!" Deputy

Campbell laughed.

"Or you could be set upon by robbers in Omaha." Sheriff Davis smiled. "Law dodgers are everywhere these days!"

They were teasing me, but I didn't mind.

"If so," I said, "you gentlemen have shown me what to do. It has been a real eye-opener for me to see what a man of firm resolution can do in the face of a bully. Or an entire mob of bullies, for all that. No, this story has had a happy ending and nothing will spoil it."

"Aye," said Deputy Campbell. "But for a' that, can I suggest to you that you go shopping for a pistol?"

As things turned out, however, it appeared that I had spoken prematurely. Our arrival in Council Bluffs did not signal a quick and happy ending to the saga of Detective Boswell. I was not only premature in saying so; I was being highly optimistic. Although the newspaper published my story — with my byline! — it soon became apparent that the narrative was not finished. Not by a long chalk. Had the pursuit and capture taken place in a big city surrounded by civilization, the jailing of Kane Kelly would have been the end of the yarn. From a secure prison cell he would have been taken to an equally secure courtroom to face trial, guarded by armed and uniformed police, and probably executed without further trouble.

But this is the West, the American frontier. Here your ordinary street bully and common scofflaw find themselves emboldened by a singularly powerful accomplice: the landscape. Here the unfenced, open country itself invites disregard for all rules of trespass and theft. If a man finds something "on the prairie," as the mountain men say, he feels free to take it. Where he chooses to go, he goes. It is commonly assumed that this unpopulated expanse must be filled with dangerous animals and hostile Indians; therefore, the bully may carry weapons openly and brandish them with impunity. It is a risk-filled region: a man is respected for his skill with a gun and his craftiness in taking whatever he wants. If the way he does it happens to incur the wrath of some small community, escape is as simple as making pie.

This was no longer true in the case of Kane Kelly himself, who by now was much subdued and feeling little except self-pity. However, his two brothers were still out there and would not hesitate to set their hands against the brash — and lone —

detective who stood in their way. They knew they could rescue their brother and get away with him, and they knew that the frontier would be their ally. Even a pistol ball in his leg would not deter Clifton Kelly.

Imagine that a man has beaten another man in a bar fight, or has assaulted a woman or stolen a horse. Perhaps he has robbed someone either by stealth or at gunpoint. Perhaps a *posse comitias* is gathering together in order to punish him. The perpetrator sees that there is no jail where they can keep him and no salaried constable to guard him from escaping. Looking outward from the edge of the little huddle of buildings called a "town," he sees the endless rolling hills. He has a gun and a horse and with these he can make his way. He can vanish into the wilderness where the committee, fettered by household and employment, lacks the will to pursue. Or the western frontier offers the rogue another route of escape: the great, unpopulated Missouri River. With a stolen boat, he could float unobserved for days downstream. On horseback he could ride upstream all the way to the great shining mountains. He has the tools of survival, the horse and gun, knife and tomahawk. The land gives him instant refuge in all directions.

In a city his horse and weapons would be of little help to him. In a city, any place of refuge would also be open to the danger of discovery. His sleep would be troubled by fears of being robbed or beaten. But in the vast emptiness of the West he can go unseen, if he wants to, unchallenged and unknown.

The freedom of the wild, however, comes with a certain price. If a man is going to live in the wilderness alone, the wilderness will require that he give up his civilized behavior and adopt the ways of the savage. If he stays long enough, his city clothes will fall apart and he will be wearing animal skins. To remain hidden he will build no house, but will sleep in caves and thickets. When powder and lead are exhausted, he will kill small animals with a club for his food; he will own nothing but what he can carry in his hands. And there is one final aspect to this price. If he decides to quit that life and return to someplace where men are building a society together, he will not be the same as when he left. If he has survived, he will be even stronger and more self-centered and scornful of city civilities. He may live among men, but he will not be part of them.

In my opinion, I was seeing just such a man in our encounters with Clifton Kelly.

He was not particularly brave, nor stalwart and heroic. His face reminded me of a rat's and, like a rat, he stayed out of sight at society's edge. He had learned how to take what he needed and he scorned anyone who was weak enough to be robbed by him. He exploited workers at every turn. He manipulated public figures. And he did it all by manipulation and cunning, seldom getting into a confrontation with his victim. Like a rat, he was only brave and aggressive when cornered. If someone posed a serious threat to him, he merely moved to a new place somewhere else on the frontier.

Learning that his brother was now languishing in the Council Bluffs jail and that Sheriff Davis and Deputy Marshal Campbell had returned to their homes, Clifton Kelly became determined to free Kane Kelly. I think it is the case that he simply saw nothing to deter the two of them from continuing to run their very profitable contracting business. Out there where there was no town, no citizens, nobody except their own paid employees, they felt free to do whatever they liked, so long as they could tell the railroad owners that the work was progressing. Out there they could beat a lazy worker, banish a man to the prairie for insubordination, shoot Indians, wage war on the herds of bison, take what they wanted from homesteaders so long as it was for the good of the great railroad system. Why should one Association detective be allowed to stand in their way?

Mr. Boswell's reply to this was always the same: "because we can." The famed American battle flag bears a dangerous serpent with the motto "Don't Tread on Me," and the standard of the Rocky Mountain Detective Association could well be a defenseless person showing the legend "Don't Tread on *Them.*" Mr. Boswell loved to see justice accomplished and bullies thwarted. The secretive network of law officers, vigilantes and paladins gave him an ideal outlet for that passion.

Once again Mr. Boswell turned to the shadowy alliance for assistance with the prisoner. It came in the shape of a young Association recruit whose name was John Day. Young Mr. Day's first job was to stay in the jail guarding Kane Kelly in order that Mr. Boswell could go across to the city's bank, where he exchanged Association chits for ready cash money. Returning to the jail, he presented young Day with the money and asked him to procure a rifle and such other weapons as might be needed in case Kelly's supporters should attack.

Mr. Boswell was delighted with the practicality of John Day's purchases. Besides their pistols, the two men were now armed with a heavy Winchester rifle in .45 caliber, as well as one of the newer model Greener breech-loading shotguns and a plentiful supply of ammunition. The lad had done so well with his bargaining that he had money left over for dried meat and ship's biscuit sufficient to last a week if necessary. Arrangements having been made with the jailer to use a small upstairs room for sleeping, Mr. Boswell and John Day settled into a routine of taking turns watching Kelly. The cell adjacent to Kelly's was vacant, so while one of them slept upstairs, the other man slept in the empty cell, the Winchester rifle and Greener shotgun by his side.

CHAPTER 5

The reader will not be surprised to learn that I went back across the river — several times — in the following days. I could not leave the story alone, despite the fact that I had sufficient "leads" on stories in Omaha to keep me busy. I much preferred to sit with Detective Boswell, either in the upstairs room or in the cell adjacent to Kelly, and listen to his stories about the Rocky Mountain Detective Association.

"You never did tell me how the Association got involved with the Madalone case," I said one day.

Mr. Boswell had his chair tilted back against the wall and had just finished loading his briar pipe. He jerked his thumb toward the sleeping figure in the next cell.

"Kane can blame his brother Sligo for that," he said. "He's a lot like Clifton. They live among decent people, yet don't seem to have the faintest understanding of how to get along with them. In the due course of time, Kane would have been tried for the shooting and might have gone to prison for a number of years. And justly so. Sligo and Clifton obviously don't believe in their brother's innocence. They just don't see why they can't do what they want."

He lit his pipe.

"Kane was in jail almost immediately after murdering Charlie," Boswell continued. "Not a safe place for him to be, but probably safer than being out of jail. Part of the crowd at Fort Steele wanted to lynch him. Part of them kept remembering that he signed the pay chits and wanted to let 'the law' deal with him so they wouldn't have to take sides. Funny, isn't it? Even out here in the West you find people who hide in their houses and want to let some constable or marshal do their work for them.

"Anyway, news of the murder finally reached Charlie's family in Colorado. They were in disbelief that he could have been killed like that. Details were sketchy. The telegram from Charlie's friends just said *Charlie Madalone killed. Wages dispute. Buried Fort Steele, Wyoming. Belongings to follow. Deep regrets.*

"As it happened, Charlie's family had a neighbor who knew General Cook, our founder and leader in the Rocky Mountain Detective Association. This neighbor asked the general if the detective network could find out more details about the case. The family had no money to pay for a detective; they simply wanted information. And General Cook agreed to find out what he could.

"Now let's take the story back to Fort Steele," Detective Boswell went on. "Clifton and Sligo were spending their evenings drinking in a saloon, cursing their brother's situation and dreaming up various dim-witted plans for a jailbreak. Half drunk and ranting about it one night, their befuddled brains somehow got hold of the notion that the US Army might get involved. The railroad being a federal project, you know. The inebriated brothers managed to convince one another that the army might ship Kane off to a federal jail somewhere, making their jailbreak plan more complicated. Then they got a brilliant idea. There *was* something they could do.

"They could go directly to Charlie's family and get them to ask the Wyoming judge to drop the charges. It would make everything very simple! Just drop the charges!

"One of the brothers — Sligo — volunteered to take a couple of men and go to Colorado. He would find the Madalone

99

family and tell them some kind of story that would seem to exonerate Kane from the murder. Make it sound like an accident or fight or something and offer them a cash settlement. Maybe he'd tell the family that he and his pals were eyewitnesses. The family hadn't talked to anybody else who had been there, so they'd believe anything they were told. Sligo would get them to sign a document freeing the contractor company from all responsibility. With such a document, they could get Kane out of jail.

"If this seems like a far-fetched idea to you, you are right. But then if you were to toss the Kelly boys into a smart pool they wouldn't rise to the top any time soon. Too much cheap alcohol has pickled their brains, in my opinion.

"So, to return to Colorado. General Cook asked me to uncover the facts surrounding the killing of Charlie and talk to the Madalones about it, so I had met the family and they knew me. One blustery afternoon the father came to my lodgings with news. Sligo Kelly and a pair of toughs had appeared in town with some kind of an offer. They were going to meet with him that same evening at the Madalone house.

"I immediately took Mr. Madalone to General Cook and apprised him of the development. I was hardly surprised when the general said that we needed more information, more details. His success as a detective has always stemmed from his meticulous accumulation of facts. Sometimes all it takes to disarm a desperate lawbreaker is to know the man's background and the facts of his case. Even an entire gang can be calmed down if you know enough personal information about some of them.

"The general therefore suggested that Mr. Madalone meet these gentlemen on his front porch. 'Do not allow them into the house,' he said. 'Give them some reason, such as a sick child who is sleeping. Detective Boswell will conceal himself beside the house where he can eavesdrop on your conversation and find out what they want.' He went on to suggest that Mr. Madalone arrange for Sligo and his confederates to return the next afternoon for more discussion. This would give us time to consider a strategy.

"Returning to the house, Mr. Madalone and I considered several hiding places near the front porch before settling on a latticework screen heavily overgrown with wild rose. Mr. Madalone would try to keep the visitors at that end of the porch so I could hear what was said. I went back to my lodgings for two revolvers, had a bit of supper, and was in my hiding place a half hour before Sligo and the boys arrived.

"Sligo began with a rough, awkward set piece of speech about how sorry they all were about Charlie's death. Sweet boy, full of promise, never hurt anybody, the sort of sentiments you might hear at a funeral. Then he came around to how his brother was in jail, that no one knew what to do next. These unfortunate accidents happen in end-of-track camps, he said. Kane is the boss contractor, and without him there's many a man out of work, not knowing what needs doing. The law in Fort Steele just wants it over with, so everything can get back to normal. On and on he went, making the murder seem like an unavoidable accident, using all the Irish in him to make a sad, sad case for Kane and all those poor, poor workmen waiting to go back to work. Nothing would bring Charlie back. No use in dwelling on it.

"Mr. Madalone finally interrupted all this blarney. 'I'm not sure what I can do about it,' he said.

"As Mr. Madalone told it to me later, Sligo reached into a coat pocket and drew out a folded document. 'Our company lawyer drew up a paper,' Sligo said. 'You sign it — we three sign as witness — then we can get on back to work and all will be well.'

"Mr. Madalone countered by giving the paper a cursory glance before putting it into his own pocket.

" 'I'll need to show it to the family,' he said.

"From my hiding place I heard — or rather did *not* hear — an awkward silence. It was obvious that Sligo didn't know what to do next. He shouldn't have let go of that document. It was Mr. Madalone who finally spoke.

" 'Did all three of you know Charlie?' he asked. 'Did you see what happened? Our lad was a fine boy, a fine boy.'

" 'No,' Sligo said. 'No, we didn't know your boy. We work on a branch line. Kelly Contracting Company, it has any number of jobs goin' on at once. Myself, I'm supervisor on a crew, just like my two brothers.'

" 'Keeps you hopping, then,' Mr. Madalone suggested.

" 'You've hit the truth there,' Sligo said.

" 'Don't know how you had time to come all this way to see us,' Mr. Madalone said.

" 'I won't say it was convenient, for certain. I can leave a man in charge, but with payday coming up and the railroad sending inspectors and all that I'm champing at the bit t'get back to work.'

" 'You boys are probably enjoying a break, though,' Mr. Madalone said to the other two toughs.

"They hemmed and hawed a moment. I heard somebody — probably one of the thugs — shuffle his boots on the porch. One of them finally found his voice.

" 'Kinda,' he admitted.

" 'You're bosses too, then?'

" 'Nah. We're kinda . . .'

"Sligo interrupted at this point.

" 'The boys got promoted off the rail gang, y' see. Now they help out with enforcement, keeping everything running smooth.'

"Aha, I thought. So Sligo is nervous about being away from his crew. And with two of his policemen as well. We might be able to do something with that."

According to Detective Boswell, when the three men had left the Madalone house, having agreed to return the next day for a decision, General Cook and Detective Boswell met with the family in the parlor. General Cook outlined his suggestions.

"First," he said, "you need not think these Kelly thugs can do anything for you, Mr.

Madalone. You will be better served by letting the Association deal with it. We have an operative near Fort Steele who can arrange the return of Charlie's effects and who can collect any money coming to him. He can even sell that pony for you and forward the money to you. You don't need Kelly. Second, all this business of a signed document to free Kane Kelly from jail is pure blarney. But . . Sligo's little brain is convinced that if he gets you to sign, then he can get back to his crew before it falls apart. If he's supervising a job and needs those two brawny lads to help keep the boys in line, it means his hold over his men is probably slippery.

"If you will trust us, Detective Boswell and me, I think we can send Sligo Kelly packing tomorrow. Afterward we'll see what we can do about making Kane Kelly pay for the murder of your boy."

Late the following afternoon General Cook and Detective Boswell went back to the Madalone house, where they joined Mr. Madalone on the front porch.

"The more I think about it, the madder I get!" Mr. Madalone said. "This railroad contractor shoots and kills our boy and thinks he can just get us to sign a paper saying we forgive him and all is well. I see red every time I think of it! And poor Charlie lying in a grave in some godforsaken place in Wyoming. General, if it takes every last damned dime I ever earn, I'll go up there and kill that Kane Kelly myself! I can't live with knowing he's gone off scot-free, no sir!"

"I am in your corner completely," the general replied. "Kane Kelly needs to face a proper judge, however. He and those who would set him free, they all need to be taught a lesson about the law of these United States. No, it won't do to simply shoot him. He and his brothers and his thugs must be put before a jury. There they will learn what trouble they bring upon themselves when they try to trample on the innocent."

"General, I just don't know what to do," Mr. Madalone said. "I can't up and leave for Wyoming, not with my family to support. And our savings are awful meager. To tell the truth, I don't even know how I'm going to pay you for your service to us."

"Ah!" the general said. "That's precisely why we have come earlier than expected, to discuss it with you. The Rocky Mountain Detective Association has done considerable service for any number of persons in Colorado. Some months ago we helped a widow lady recover her mineral rights from a pair of criminals. She had lost her husband and her son in a mining explosion. We recovered a considerable fortune for her. In return, she offered to use part of her money to help the Association, should a worthy case arise. Yesterday evening I visited her. She feels deep pity for your loss, and even deeper sympathy. She agrees with me that your son's murder should be resolved. She offers to cover all of the Association expenses connected with it. All expenses."

"What?" Mr. Madalone exclaimed. "Why, that's a miracle, a holy miracle! How could we accept, though? If she'd do this for Charlie . . how we'd ever thank her I don't know. Truly I don't. I'll find a way to pay her back, I will. However long it takes. What a fine thing to do. A fine thing."

"It goes further," General Cook continued. "In her generosity and gratefulness, the same lady wishes to underwrite the expenses of Detective Boswell if he will travel up to Wyoming and see that justice is done to Kane Kelly for the murder of your boy. What do you think? Shall we set Boswell on the trail? I assure you, he is a bulldog when he gets hold of a case such as this."

Just then they saw Sligo and his two accomplices coming down the walk.

"I think we will, and with eternal thanks to you," Mr. Madalone whispered. "Yes, by God, I think we will!"

"Very well," the general said. "Then follow my lead for the next few minutes and we will see whether we can stir up a hornet's nest with these boys."

Sligo's boys waited at the walk as Sligo came up the steps onto the porch. He glared at the two detectives standing by the front door and addressed Mr. Madalone without looking at him.

"And who do we have here?" Sligo demanded.

"I am David Cook of the Rocky Mountain Detective Association. This is Detective Boswell."

"What are you doing here?" Sligo said.

"We are friends of Charlie Madalone's family," General Cook replied. "And we are here to give advice and to protect his interests."

"Well!" snarled the ugly face. "As it happens, so am I. I gave him a document for his signature. I advise Madalone to sign it. In his own best interest."

"Let me see it."

The paper in question was produced, whereupon General Cook unfolded it and quickly read through it. He handed it to

108

Mr. Boswell.

"What do you think of this, Detective?"

Mr. Boswell gave it a quick read. It was two pages of nonsense larded with legalistic terms such as "party of the first part" and "in consideration herewith" and "unqualified exoneration." There was even a mention of *habeas corpus* in it. All in all, it seemed to have been written by a drunken lawyer, and not one who had graduated top of his class. It was utter nonsense and would never be recognized by any court of law as a legitimate document.

"It seems in order," said General Cook, passing the paper to Mr. Madalone. "I suggest you get your pen and sign it. Do you agree, Mr. Boswell?"

"I agree."

Mr. Madalone went into the house and returned with a pen and ink. He signed the paper, whereupon General Cook took it and signed as witness, making his signature with a dramatic flourish, then presented it to Mr. Boswell to do the same. But he did not let go of it. After the detective had signed as second witness, General Cook made a grand show of blowing the ink dry. Then he folded the paper and put it in his inside pocket. As he opened his coat to gain access to his pocket, he revealed the shoulder holster and revolver he carried.

"What the . . . ?" Sligo grumbled. "Give that to me. What are you doing?"

"A man of your legal acumen?" the general replied. "Surely you know that you could not deliver this legal paper to a district judge *yourself,* in person! Why, the judge would ask you to prove that you came by it legitimately. He would insist on proof that it is not a forgery. For you to carry this back to Wyoming . . . Why, it would be like the prisoner writing it in his cell and handing it through the bars. No, no. Nothing will do except to have Detective Boswell deliver it. A disinterested third party, you see. The Association will do it for you, and free of charge. The detective will travel to Wyoming and present the document to the proper authority. At the same time he can collect Charlie's personal effects and settle the matter of the pony."

Sligo sputtered and argued, but finally had no show at all. It looked to him as though the detectives were serious, since they had signed his piece of paper, and that they were legitimate officers acting on Madalone's behalf. The matter had been taken out of his hands, and he was obviously torn between being extremely irritated and glad that he could get back to bossing his track gang. And he could tell his brother that the wheels of his release from jail had been set in motion.

"It was an ideal situation for a law officer," Detective Boswell said. He opened a pen knife and gave the bowl of his pipe a meticulous scraping. "Sligo thought he had succeeded, but had actually failed and would learn so as soon as he returned without the signed document. He had left his job, gone to considerable expense, and achieved nothing. And now, of course, the brothers would need a new plan for getting our prisoner out of jail."

"General Cook seems to be a good man," I said. "Once the Madalone matter is settled, I would like to write the history of the Rocky Mountain Detective Association. How did he come to be called 'General' Cook, do you know?"

"Yes," Mr. Boswell replied. "He entered the law as a young man, acting as a detective and then a sheriff in Colorado during the mining boom. His integrity and skill as a leader came to the attention of the territorial government, and he was appointed major general of the Colorado Militia. He likes to joke that they gave him a title in lieu of a salary. It is not so prestigious a title as it would be in the regular army, but it seems to fit him very well. It's rather like calling a southern gentleman 'Colonel' so-and-so."

CHAPTER 6

It probably took a full week for word to get back to Sligo and Clifton Kelly that their brother was now languishing in a jail at Council Bluffs on the edge of the Missouri River. You can imagine their frustration. At any moment Detective Boswell might take the prisoner onto a ferry boat, cross the river to Omaha and board a train for Wyoming. Probably angered by Sligo's ineptitude and undoubtedly annoyed at having to deal with the Kane problem rather than running the contracting business, Clifton rushed to Council Bluffs to effect a rescue.

He would, however, be at a great disadvantage there, for in Council Bluffs the Kellys had no employees, no gang to face the detective's determination and revolvers. Clifton sought out one of the grubbiest of the town's watering holes — his natural habitat — in the hope that a few shots of whiskey would help him to come up with a plot to save Kane. As it happened, Clifton was being watched by another man, a man of natural curiosity, a man whom I would later interview for my story.

The night wore on. The level of whiskey in the bottles went lower and lower. At a table adjacent to Clifton Kelly, four men were becoming louder and ruder with each passing glass. According to my informant, they were your below-average low-life sort, drifters who could work hard but who couldn't tolerate being told what to do. No job ever seems to suit such men for long, so they migrate from town to town, from job to job, and from tavern to saloon. At present they were loudly congratulating one another for assaulting their former foreman. They toasted one another as splendid fellows and excellent men, men who should not be required to put up with any foreman's unfair censure.

"By God," one of them slurred as he made a drunken search through his pockets, "boys, I'm tapped! But listen: if I had only a dollar left, by God, I'd buy all you a drink. All of you! That's the kind of pal I am, use my last dollar to buy pals a drink. By God."

Hearing this, Clifton Kelly suddenly had a magnificent idea. Picking up his own half-empty whiskey bottle, he moved his chair to their table and set the bottle down.

"Have some of mine," he said.

And they thanked him and drank his health. He drank their health. They again returned the compliment. Clifton signaled the barkeep to bring a fresh bottle. When he felt the moment was right, he made his pitch.

"Boys," he said, "I'm needin' some help. Might call it temporary assistance. Take an hour, no more. I'd pay twenty dollars to each man for it, too."

One of them seemed to be calculating how much liquor twenty dollars would buy. All four leaned in toward Kelly like conspirators to hear the details.

"Got a brother," Kelly said in confidential tones. "Right here in your town. Some damn Denver detective wants to take m'brother to Laramie so's they can hang 'im. Hang 'im!"

This caused a general uproar of indignation and prompted a round of toasts to the absent brother.

"Not even a lawman," Clifton continued. "Damn detective. He's got m'brother over in that jailhouse. Locked up."

"I been in there, that jail!" one of the four exclaimed. "Dark as hell. God, it's a dark place. Constable used to leave a lamp

115

burnin' at night, but it'd always run out of oil. Dark as hell."

"No guards?"

"Hell, no. Got these cells, see? Iron cages. A man's got no show t'break out. Night comes, they lock that big front door too — heavy ol' door, two locks on it, go home t'their beds. Leave a man shiverin' in the damn dark all night."

"Dammit!" Kelly exclaimed. The others echoed this fine sentiment and drank Clifton's health again.

"Listen," he said. "Gotta get m'brother outa there. That detective, he knows me, see? He'll see me comin' and not let me near the place. Probably shoot me like he did my other brother. Did I tell y' he already shot me once? But that Denver man don't know you fellows. Have yourselfs 'nother drink here."

Clifton's face took on the sly look of the fox in the fairy tales.

"Twenty dollars, American. If you boys jus' knew where t'get hold of some tools. You boys go over there with some tools, see? Y' bust that door open, come back with m'brother. Then him and me, we'll be long gone by first light and you boys'll have twenty dollars each. Don't worry about that damn detective. He don't know you and

116

don't know the town. Never know who done it, see? Never catch up with you. Twenty dollars."

To show his honesty, Clifton Kelly put four gold pieces on the table for them to see. The four looked into one another's bloodshot eyes, nodded at one another like puppets, and stood up.

"By God, mister," said the spokesman, "you jus' get your horses ready and we'll be right back. Jus' gonna stop off at th' rail yard tool shack. No problem for us to swipe a pick and sledgehammer, eh boys? And b'fore y'can say Jack Rosilyn we'll have your good ol' brother back in the bosom of his . . well, we'll bring him."

With that, according to my informant, the four tough-looking gents sallied forth on their mission of mercy.

The four-man whiskey posse came to the jail carrying a stolen sledgehammer, a longhorn pick and a pry bar. They arrived expecting to find the place dark and deserted, but it was not quite dark; a lantern hung above the door, throwing a circle of light on the ground in front of the doorway. A gleam of light also showed through the small viewing grill in the door.

Three of the Kelly rescuers held back a

few feet and urged their comrade with the sledgehammer to step forward and take a swing at the thick door. Filled with more whiskey than judgment, he agreed that it was exactly the right way to begin.

"Watch this," he slurred. "I bet I bust that ol' door wide open, one good hit'll do 'er. Shtand back."

But no sooner had he raised that hammer and stepped toward the door than, to the amazement of all four drunks, the door swung back on its own. They saw a lantern sitting on the floor inside, shielded so as to throw light out the door but not back into the building. Except for that bright lantern, all was dark within. The hammer bearer stepped back in confused surprise. He needed to smash that door, but now the door was wide open and it bewildered him.

A firm (and sober) voice boomed from the darkness of the building. "What do you want?"

There was jostling and pushing among the drunks as a spokesman was selected. This individual steadied himself with the long-horn pick, leaning on it like a cane to keep himself vertical. He cleared his throat and spoke up. "We come for whassis name! Mur-phy!"

"Kelly," his comrade corrected.

"Kelly!"

"You can't have him. And you're drunk. Go find somewhere and sleep it off."

"Nossir! Gotta get Kelly," the pick man said. "Man sent us."

"His brother, no doubt. Ugly man in a green vest? Face like a constipated fox? He walked with a bad limp?"

"Yessir, that's thim. Him."

"He limps like that because I shot him."

"Oh."

"Still gotta get Kelly," one of them said. "You alone in there, huh?"

The detective began to find the conversation boring. Boring and pointless. He raised his rifle. There was the sudden explosive *crack* of a heavy Winchester. The lead slug screamed from the doorway to shatter the pick handle, sending splinters in all directions. As you would expect, this had a sobering effect on the man who stood there holding the remains of the handle. The pick was ruined; and when the Winchester spoke a second time, *crack,* the sledgehammer went the way of the pick, becoming a ten-pound lump of malleable steel with no visible handle.

The Winchester's roar was deafening. As gun smoke rolled toward them on the night breeze, the quartet retreated backward like petitioners parting from the king's presence. Once they reached the darkness outside the circle of lantern light, they broke and ran, presumably to find the saloon again. Or, more wisely, a different saloon.

With the idea of a direct assault stymied, Clifton Kelly would stumble upon a way to launch a more subtle and devious attack upon Detective Boswell, this one all the more dangerous because it could not be answered with a Winchester rifle. It would threaten Mr. Boswell's character and reputation. I wish I could have been on hand to witness what followed. But as things turned out, Mr. Boswell and I shared many long hours of travel together, during which he became unusually eager to talk about this experience. Uncharacteristically eager.

As I have said, Clifton Kelly was more or less a stranger in Council Bluffs and had no employees in that city. The four ruffians he tried to hire told and retold their story in local saloons, displaying the shattered pick handle for its dramatic effect on the listeners. As their story of Boswell's bravery and marksmanship grew and spread, Kelly found that he could not engage even a single thug who would be willing to spring his brother from jail. It was widely believed, at least in the more alcoholic circles, that this new detective in town could hit a two-bit piece at two hundred yards and that he never slept. No one knew how many deputies he might have with him. No, the politic thing was to ignore Mr. Clifton Kelly, even if he did pay for whiskey.

But one fine morning, having breakfast at the boardinghouse where he had taken a room, Clifton happened to fall into conversation with an accomplice who *was* desperate enough to approach Boswell and free the prisoner. It was sheer coincidence. As the plot formed in his mind, Kelly chuckled to himself at his own cleverness. He would outwit the detective and outmaneuver him. With any luck, he might even succeed in destroying Boswell's credibility.

CHAPTER 7

The excitement began on a warm afternoon. Later on as he helped me fill in the details of the story, Mr. Boswell said that every moment of that afternoon was etched into his memory.

John Day was at his post in the jail downstairs, the Greener shotgun across his knees and his revolver loose in its holster. Kane Kelly snored away in his cell. Upstairs in the small sleeping room, Detective Boswell was lying on the cot and sleeping lightly, resting himself until he would take over the watch.

The sound of feet upon the stairway woke Mr. Boswell instantly, although it was a very slight sound indeed. Someone was coming up the steps and someone — or something — was brushing against the wall of the stairwell. Faster than thought, Mr. Boswell was on his feet with his revolver in hand. Someone had gotten past young John downstairs; he could only imagine that whoever it was had rendered John helpless in some manner. But why had they not freed the prisoner and made off? Maybe Kelly's brother had lost the remainder of his patience and had decided to kill the detective and rid himself of the problem.

There came a light knocking at the door.

"Mr. Boswell?"

It was a woman's voice. Boswell remained silent and listening until he was confident that she was alone on the landing.

"Mr. Boswell?" the voice came again.

The detective lowered his revolver and opened the door two inches, keeping his foot against it.

"Yes?"

"May I speak with you?"

He opened the door all the way. She was indeed alone out on the stair landing.

Her eyes, a kind of deep amber like polished agate, regarded him without a hint of shyness or uncertainty. The little slant of her head and suggestion of a raised eyebrow indicated that she was curious about him. Even in the gloomy shadows of the landing, Detective Boswell could see he was face-to-face with that rare phenomenon, an attractive woman who could make a man's pulse beat harder simply by looking at him. Men would find themselves unable to stop looking back at her, their brains held in a fascination which they could not explain. No doubt other women also regarded her with interest, envying her genteel poise, her self-confident bearing. Her hair was carefully brushed and symmetrically parted, swept back into a tidy knot behind. Her dress consisted of a wide, full skirt — which accounted for the brushing sound he had heard coming up the stairway — with tailored bodice and full sleeves. The material was silk, so deeply brown as to look almost black. The skirt had no visible pockets, so if she had come to his room in order to shoot him and was carrying a gun about her, it would be in the small purse she had in one hand, although it was so little that it could hardly hold so much as a derringer.

"Come in," Mr. Boswell said.

He offered her the only chair in the small room. As for himself, he chose to stand next to the window, where he could watch the alley below. It was obvious why John Day had admitted this woman to the jail building; she was mistress of a demeanor that would cause any man to grant her wishes without being asked. Her posture was that of a royal princess. She took her seat on the

124

simple wooden chair as though it were a throne. Mr. Boswell noticed she did not perform the gestures so many women do when seating themselves: the arranging of skirts and the shuffling of feet and the fluttering of the hands coming to rest upon the lap and all of that. This creature seated herself and was perfection. The agate eyes confronted his and she addressed him with candid directness.

"I am Elisabeth Greene," she said. "My husband was Colonel Hubert Greene. He was killed during an action in the Kansas Territory two years ago. I now live in Council Bluffs."

"How do you do?" said Mr. Boswell. "My sympathies on the loss of your husband. I wonder . . do I need to introduce myself? Something tells me it would be unnecessary."

"You are correct," the woman replied. "I was told about you, Detective. However, I will say they described a somewhat different man than you appear to be. I was led to expect a gruff, more primitive fellow. The kind of cigar-chewing, overweight individual one sometimes finds working as detectives in city hotels. I now see that image does not fit you. You seem to be a gentleman. Not young, but in no sense could you be called old."

And so she was candid as well as beautiful.

"Thank you," said Mr. Boswell. Uncomfortable and wishing to change the direction of the conversation, he returned to the original topic.

"It must be difficult for you as a widow," he said. "Are there children, or do you live alone?"

"All alone, I'm afraid," she said. "I have rooms at a local boardinghouse, and I act as a private tutor for a number of children. Between that and the army pension, I manage to get by. But as you say, it is difficult at times."

Detective Boswell adjusted the curtain to provide himself with a better view of the alley behind the building. This woman was a charming widow, but it would not do to let down his guard and allow any ruffians to sneak up on the back door. It was still possible she had been sent as a distraction for such a maneuver.

"But to come to my point," Elisabeth Greene continued. "Yesterday a certain Mr. Kelly approached me — he happens to have a room in the boardinghouse where I live — and told me the sad story of his brother's plight. His brother is wounded, I understand? And is arrested and being held prisoner, but not by a — excuse me for saying it — not by a credentialed law officer."

"Yes, but that's not the entire . ."

"He told me all about the misunderstanding leading to the death of that poor boy in Wyoming. A terrible accident. The boy's parents have every right to be upset. I, myself, lost a child to the influenza epidemic and I know the pain of such sorrow."

Mr. Boswell wanted to set the woman straight about the case; but an inner shield interposed itself in his mind, warning him that it would be more prudent to drop it. Instead, he murmured a few words of sympathy and allowed her to go on.

"Before you say anything," she continued, "I know I have heard only one side of the story. In my situation it does not matter, at least not to me. That's not why I came to see you. I suspect that you are not a man who tolerates being lied to, Mr. Boswell, so I will tell you the truth about why I'm here. I will place all my trust in your sense of justice. While I do manage to eke out an existence here in Council Bluffs, my dream is to return to Philadelphia where I have friends and relations. Mr. Kelly has offered me one thousand dollars, money I sorely need. Please don't misunderstand; I would like to remain in the West and perhaps have a farm. The freedom and fresh air are most appealing to me. I'd love to be able to raise my own vegetables and keep a yard for poultry. Instead of living in a city I would prefer to have a porch with a view of hills and fields. I would like to sit by my own hearth of an evening. But as you heard, when I introduce myself, it is as a struggling widow. My whole identity is dictated by being a struggling widow woman. Back east, with the support of my city relatives, I would be able to become someone other than that. Do you know what I'm saying?"

Mr. Boswell searched the bold eyes, took note of the very faint blush on the perfect cheekbones. He was still somewhat non-plussed to have such a woman seated in his room. And she had come to him because Kelly had offered her money. But to do what? Surely she was not suggesting . .

"I'm not sure I catch your meaning, no."

"Out here I'm 'the widow lady' who tutors. Back east I could possibly find a career or even a new marriage. My cousins would see to it that I got back into polite society and met people."

"I see. This explains why you need Kelly's money."

"I would never have agreed to Mr. Kelly's suggestion, were it not for the money. Please understand. I am extremely reluctant to become involved in anything involving crime and violence. However, Mr. Boswell, this might be my one chance to quit the West and go back to somewhere I could belong. I did not mind following my husband out here, because it was for the good of his career. And I found myself loving the beauty of the prairies and hills. But with the Colonel gone, I cannot stay. This money could mean everything to me."

"Did Kelly pay you in advance?"

"Half. Half of the money is now safe in the bank. The rest depends upon whether I can persuade you."

"Persuade me? To do what, exactly?"

"Please hear me out. Mr. Kelly knows that you are preparing to cross the river and proceed to Laramie City with his brother. He has contacted some friends of his brother — employees, I believe they are — who will meet the train somewhere west of Omaha. Some small water stop or station. These friends will wait there. The plan is that, in some peaceful and casual manner, Kane Kelly will quietly pass out of your custody and into theirs. Mr. Kelly promises that his brother and he will go back to being honest and productive citizens. Whether I believe him does not matter. What I do think matters is that he and his brother provide employment for dozens of men and contribute to the economy of several towns along several railroad construction routes. It would be a shame for him to continue in your custody and deny jobs to all those workers. Mr. Kelly is prepared to spend a great deal of money to liberate his brother. You and I both know, of course, that a long legal process would drain the company's resources."

"So," the detective said, "I just give over Kane Kelly? I release him? Then what do I do? Should I proceed to the judge at Laramie City and say that Kane escaped, or some such thing?"

"That part is up to you."

"And what do I get out of it?"

"Nothing. According to Mr. Kelly, you have a strong reputation for incorruptibility; therefore, no bribe of any sort will be offered. Not to you."

"Not to me? Then to whom?"

"To the boy's family. Mr. Kelly is prepared to negotiate the amount, but he offers the Madalone family not less than ten thousand dollars. He reckons it as the approximate cost of mounting a legal defense, coupled with the loss of time and business. This money will be given to you, and you will deliver it to the unfortunate family of the boy who was killed. It is not blood money, nor does it reflect any feelings of guilt. Mr. Kelly sees it as fair compensation for an accident sustained by a company employee."

Mr. Boswell sat without moving or speaking. It was a bald-faced, bold move by Clifton Kelly. In fact, it was more masterful than Kelly himself probably realized. The detective could refuse outright, thus disappointing the needy widow and reawakening Kelly's anger. Those men who would be waiting for him west of Omaha could very well take Kane Kelly by force anyway, perhaps killing someone in the process, and there would be no money for Charlie's family. And nothing could prevent Clifton Kelly from taking back his money from Elisabeth Greene, by force if he had to.

The detective was tempted to agree to this outrageous "offer" if for no other reason than to see Mrs. Elisabeth Greene out of harm's way and on her way to Philadelphia. She did not know how treacherous and dangerous Kelly could be. He had to help her and he wanted to help her. No matter how he did it, however, it could come at the cost of his own reputation. Or hers. If she went back to Clifton and told him she had failed, he might threaten her with physical harm. At the very least his refusal could cause an ugly scene in the boardinghouse for her.

As for his own reputation . . He didn't know about Clifton Kelly, but Kane Kelly would certainly publish the report that Detective Boswell of the Rocky Mountain Detective Association had taken a bribe, no matter what he did with the money. If he took the money and later went back on his word to release Kane, they would certainly spread the word that Boswell had taken a bribe and was not to be trusted.

What was he to do?

First and foremost, Detective Boswell would adhere to the truth. Mrs. Greene was clearly too intelligent to be lied to; but above that, honesty was simply one of Mr. Boswell's traits. Whatever he said from this point on would be true.

He gazed out the window as his mind methodically sifted through the facts and the various options. Finally he spoke.

"I believe you are being watched," he said.

"Oh, yes. I'm sure of it," Mrs. Greene replied. "Mr. Kelly would not want me to walk away with his money."

"We can't let you stay here, in this room

alone with me, for much longer," the detective observed. "It wouldn't be proper, for one thing. For another, Kelly might decide to use our being together as some kind of blackmail against either one of us. So, let me suggest what we do. Why don't you leave here immediately, and start to walk back to your boardinghouse. I will follow and catch you up, or failing that, I will call for you at your lodging. We'll take a long walk together and let Kelly's agent follow. I'm confident that the two of us can come up with a way to exploit this situation."

"Exploit?" she said, her eyebrow arching in a most becoming manner. "I'm not sure I care for your terminology. It sounds devious somehow."

"Excuse me. What I mean is, we can reach an agreement, come up with some sort of plan that will satisfy Kelly and will be of benefit to the both of us as well."

"That's better," she said, smiling for the first time. "The boardinghouse is at six twenty-three Pacific Street."

"It was very nice meeting you," Mr. Boswell said.

He had scarcely closed the door when his mind went into high speed. So long as Kelly thought he was considering the bribe and was interested in hearing more about it,

Mrs. Greene would be safe. Moreover, there would be no physical assault on the jail, which meant the detective was free to leave and free to talk to her. In fact, if he could manage to convince Kelly that the plan was succeeding, there would be no attempt to free the prisoner. This aspect of the situation pleased Mr. Boswell, since as a lawman, his first responsibility was to get his prisoner across the river and onto a westbound train without anyone getting injured. That was the priority. It made a little bending of the truth not only permissible but necessary.

It took some time for Detective Boswell to comb his hair and brush his clothing and to brief the deputy on the situation. When he finally reached the boardinghouse at 623 Pacific, Elisabeth Greene was standing before the mirror in the foyer. She smiled at him in the reflection, used a slender finger to tuck a stray curl of her brunette hair up under her hat, then accepted his arm to descend the front steps to the street.

"There is a pleasant little park nearby," she said. "Shall we go in that direction?"

They walked in silence for a while, her hand lying lightly on his arm. Finally she spoke.

"I imagine you would be disappointed if you do not see Kane Kelly hanged for murder," she said. "Therefore I have little hope that you will agree to his brother's terms. But before you give me your answer, I want you to know what a great pleasure it has been to meet you. I'll admit that I was frightened by the prospect of approaching you, but now I feel that we have known one another for some time. Isn't that odd?"

The detective did not reply, but not because he had nothing to say.

"I confess," he told me later on, "that walking next to that graceful lady with her hand on my arm, I wanted to blurt out that I had never met anyone like her. I wanted to say I'd do anything to have her stay in Council Bluffs. My brain was trying to find a word for what I was feeling — you're the word man, Phillip. What word am I looking for? Fluttery? Nonplussed?"

Whatever the word, he did not confess the feeling to her. Instead he steered the conversation toward something she had said earlier.

"You mentioned . . something about a farm?"

"Yes!" she said. "The Colonel and I often spoke of it. For us, returning to Philadelphia meant — means — returning to all the safe things, the same groups of people, the same entertainments, the same streets. I see myself with a small room, a small rocking chair and one of those small dogs. Tea with friends once a week. But how exciting it was for us to talk about building our own house out in the West! To raise animals and poultry, to gather our own firewood and sit by our own hearth reading books together or to walk on land that had no fences and no sidewalks."

"A nice dream," he said.

"But not terribly realistic," she replied. "Perhaps someday I can return. For now my best option — indeed, my only option — is to take the money Kelly is offering and go back to living safely among my safe people. Of course, I may not get the needed money unless you can give up your own intention. To see Kane Kelly hanged for murder, I mean."

"Hanging Kane Kelly," he said. "It won't bring the Madalone boy back to life. I am well aware of that. Moreover, the Madalone family needs the money. I have already shot and wounded both of the Kelly brothers, not to mention disrupting their contracting business. So in a sense, they've already been punished and penalized. Eleven thousand dollars more would add a considerable fine to their injury."

"And so you'll do it?" There was a note of relief and intensity in her voice. Much of her future could depend upon his answer.

"I don't like having you involved in such shady doings," he answered. "What's to prevent Clifton Kelly from cheating you, for instance?"

"I have thought of that," she said. "I have placed him in a position where it is he who has to trust *me*. The first half of my fee is already in my bank account. When I return with your answer, I will accompany him to the bank where he will deposit the remainder in the same account — *before* I inform him of the outcome of our conversation."

"Ah," said the detective. "And could you be safely out of Council Bluffs in case the Kellys came back across the river for their money? I have dealt with these men, and I fully believe they are capable of forcing you to take the money out of the bank and giving it to them."

"I have thought of that as well."

Detective Boswell was liking this woman more and more.

"I've withdrawn enough money for my trip east. The remainder will be wired to my cousin in Philadelphia. All of my belongings are already in a crate at the boardinghouse, and the owner has instructions to ship them after me. I have a travelling case packed. I am ready to catch the first eastbound train."

"Good," Mr. Boswell said. "Frankly, I will hate to see you leave. I believe we could become very good friends. However, these Kellys can be treacherous rascals. As much as I would like to see more of you, I would rather see you beyond their reach."

"To be frank in return," she said with a distracting smile, "I believe we are much alike in our thinking."

It was Mr. Boswell's turn to smile. In that simple exchange of innocent words, there was a sudden importance, a larger meaning. The mundane details of the Kelly contractors had, for that moment, fled. As he told me later, Mr. Boswell found himself trying to find a word to describe whatever it was that was passing between them.

She broke the lovely awkward silence first.

"So you'll do it? You'll be willing to go along with Mr. Kelly's scheme?"

"I want to think it through," Mr. Boswell said. "To be sure I haven't missed something. For instance — and Clifton Kelly may not have thought of this — I cannot ask any officer to accompany me from this point on. Once I cross the Missouri to Omaha, I will be alone with the prisoner.

The trip from there westward might well turn dangerous. I need a little time to consider. Besides, it is the doctor's opinion that Kane Kelly needs a few more days of recuperation from his wound."

"So what do I tell Clifton?"

"You may tell Clifton to make the arrangements. For his men to meet the train west of Omaha, I mean. You may also tell him to deposit your final payment and to get the cash payment ready for me. Tell him to make it *fifteen* thousand dollars. There are 'expenses' that have already been incurred in connection with this case, you see."

"And this means you intend to do it?" she asked. Her gaze was direct and challenging. Such eyes, Mr. Boswell thought. Why have I never noticed a woman's eyes before? How bewitching, how beautiful a woman's eyes can be!

"Kelly needs to give me time to get things ready and for the prisoner to heal a little more. Tell him we'll cross over the river during the next four days. That is, if the river doesn't rise, or if something untoward doesn't happen in the meantime. In the next four days. Then I'll wait in Omaha for the next westbound train. With the prisoner, of course."

"Very well," she said. "Thank you."

139

"Please let me know as soon as you have your money," he said.

"The money," she said. "Yes. We mustn't lose sight of the money. The money is the most important thing."

Her voice had taken on a stiff edge, which surprised him. It seemed to be communicating some sense of disappointment in the detective, and in herself. She said very little else, but clearly she believed the detective was ready to accept Kelly's bribe and would probably keep a large share for himself. Well, he could not help what she thought. To do so would spoil the game. No, when it was all over, he would try to get in touch with her and explain.

She gave him a Philadelphia address, asking him to send her a letter and tell her how the affair ended.

"You assume I'll still be alive at the end of this matter," he said, trying to act merry and nonchalant about it. "I appreciate that. Very much! I have an idea — I will give your address to my young reporter friend. If I'm unable to write to you, he will let you know how it all spun out. All right?"

"I suppose so. I am beginning to wish I could stay," she said seriously. "If only . . well, never mind. The safest course of action is to go through with my plan and not look back. As I said earlier, it could be my last chance to make a genuine change in my situation. Please know, however, that I'll miss you, even though we have only just met. I'll be worried about you until I hear that everything is all right."

Elisabeth accepted the detective's arm as they walked back to her lodgings. There she left him as cordially and with as much poise as she had shown when he first laid eyes on her. He listened to the *tap-tap-tap* of her heels crossing the walk and ascending the stairs, and in his imagination he heard again the rustle of her skirts brushing the stairway.

"All of a sudden," he told me later, "I found myself thinking that the little sleeping room above the jail cells would now feel empty, very empty somehow. I had never given that drab little room a moment's thought before. Now I did not want to see it again, not without her in it."

The waiting took more than human patience. Even more irksome to the detective was the knowledge that he and John Day were being watched at all times. Their rat-faced adversary was a distrustful, suspicious and sneaking creature. Now that he had resorted to bribery — and thought he was getting away with it — he would bribe anyone in order to protect his investment. Detective Boswell realized that Kelly's spies could be anywhere, and that his every move was probably being watched.

He had to admit that this was a complication he had not anticipated. If he tried to sneak the prisoner out of town, the word would get to his brother very quickly and an attempt on his life might follow. He had thought about arranging to be ferried across the Missouri under cover of darkness, but he could not be seen speaking with any of the men at the docks. He also thought about sending a telegraph to enlist a few dependable members of the Association to meet him at Omaha, but he would be seen going into the telegraph office and Kelly could conceivably bribe the operator to reveal what he had sent.

In the week of waiting, Detective Boswell had one bright spot of satisfaction: Elisabeth Greene. Each thought of her caused his face to relax into an involuntary smile. He liked to lie back on his cot, he told me, with his hands beneath his head, remembering her voice, her walk, her face. He could remember every detail of the little park where they had walked together.

The two of them had handled the Kelly situation perfectly, he thought. She had acquired Clifton Kelly's money without lying, and she had shipped herself and her belongings back east without difficulty. The only shadow on their success was Mr. Boswell's feelings of regret, his fear that he would never see her again. Council Bluffs seemed more grubby to him than it had before she left. He found himself imagining her train journey and her happy reunion with her relatives. He imagined what her house in Philadelphia looked like and how lovely she would appear by candlelight in a gracefully furnished drawing room. Quite elegant.

Grubby as the place seemed, there was a positive side to being in Council Bluffs. Young John Day had trustworthy cronies in the town, men who would from time to time casually meet him on some corner or in a saloon and bring him information about Clifton Kelly's movements.

"The rat kept his eye on the cheese," Detective Boswell later said, "but the cat was keeping his eye on the rat."

Around noon a week later, one of John Day's worthy comrades came running to the jail with news. Another friend of theirs, a minor clerk at the bank, reported that a "very large" sum of money had been transferred in Kelly's name and that Kelly had immediately taken it in cash. It might have been the ten-thousand-dollar bribe. Not only that, but Kelly had been seen going aboard the scheduled ferry to cross the Missouri River. He was on his way to set up the paying of the bribe and secure the release of his brother.

"Then it's time to act," said Detective Boswell, "but it might be a trick. Kelly is still treacherous. We'll need to conceal our own movements as much as possible."

John Day was dispatched to arrange for an evening crossing by private boat; the doctor was sent for to have a last look at Kane Kelly's wound; a telegram was sent over to an Omaha member of the Association, instructing him to meet them a mile upstream of the ferry landing with team and buggy, and take them by backstreets to the Omaha city jail. There Kelly would be lodged until the next train.

There was only one unexpected development, but a happy one: John Day insisted upon accompanying Detective Boswell to the other side of the river and possibly beyond. His enthusiasm and quick mind would be most welcome, of course. However, his participation would make Mr. Boswell seem to be a liar, since he said he was coming alone. Still, he doubted whether it would matter. The important thing was for Clifton Kelly to believe that "the fix was in" for his brother to be handed over once the party was clear of Omaha.

The unknown factor, of course, was Clifton Kelly's capacity for treachery.

CHAPTER 8

The Missouri River's swirls of muscled
brown water reached everywhere like long
tentacles. They pulled and pushed at the
small boat, making it tip dangerously from
side to side as the river man strained his
oars trying to stay on a straight course. The
river flowed relentlessly, as it had been doing for untold centuries, carrying its load of
silt and half-submerged debris toward the
Mississippi. To the big river the little craft
with its four humans was of no more significance than if it had been a wood chip. The
man at the oars struggled and swore with
each vagary of the thick current.

The prairie sky was still light, but the
riparian forest on the opposite shore was
like a solid black wall. At last the passengers
spotted the swinging dot of a lantern. After
every few pulls on his oars, the rower would
turn his head just long enough to get a bearing on the light. He laid into his work with

a will, eager to be done with the powerful surges and swirls of an indifferent river.

Mr. Boswell's instructions had been followed exactly. The Rocky Mountain associate on the western bank, the man with the lantern, had a good buggy and team waiting in the deep woods. He assured them that the dirt track into Omaha was clear.

"One problem, though," he said. "The jail is full. More than full, thanks to a drunken celebration the other evening. And on top of that, I believe someone is watching the jail. No idea who it is — seems to be a newcomer among the usual loiterers. Two men were released this morning, and I witnessed this individual approach them as if to ask them about the other inmates."

"I would suspect him of being a Kelly confederate," Mr. Boswell said. "We will proceed on that assumption, at least. Your suggestion, then?"

Mr. Boswell and John Day were both checking the loads on their pistols, lest the river crossing had made the powder damp.

"I have a good friend, a man whom I trust. He operates a rooming house on a street handy to the train station. At the moment he has only one lodger and can give you the entire upstairs. Three rooms. It's a sturdy building, a bit old. Narrow stairway, one exit onto the street and one into the alley."

"Excellent!" said the detective. "Let's be off!"

"I can't tell you how wonderful it felt to me to be across the Missouri at last," Detective Boswell later told me. "Stepping out onto that far shore filled me with a sense of liberation, a sensation of being free to stretch my muscles and do my duty without being watched or hindered. It was as if the West began there on the bank of the river. Omaha seemed ready to deal everyone a fresh hand in the game. My only regret was that crossing the river took me farther away from news of my new friend, Elisabeth Greene."

While John Day was helping Kane Kelly into the buggy, Mr. Boswell paid the boatman and thanked him for his service. As the money was changing hands, he realized the boatman had been standing there throughout the conversation and was now aware of their new plan. The detective cursed himself for not speaking with the associate in private. And now he had no choice but to let the boatman return to Council Bluffs where he would no doubt head for a saloon to drink and talk about his evening's work.

Damn. It probably wouldn't matter, but damn it anyway.

The rooming house was comfortable and private. They were told that they could have the top floor all to themselves; the detective chose the most secure room, had a third cot brought in and, after a good supper of cold corned beef and cabbage, they lay down for a much-needed rest. Kane Kelly was a tired, subdued man and offered only mild protests as his ankle was being shackled to the bed frame.

Detective Boswell was the first to awake the next morning. All was in good order: John Day was stirring and stretching beneath the blanket; Kane Kelly lay flat on his back, snoring with a noise that reminded Mr. Boswell of a tin bucket being bumped down the sides of a well shaft.

Mr. Boswell washed and dressed, waking John Day in the process, and the sounds of their boots on the floor brought the landlord bearing a pot of coffee and hot sausages and bread. While eating, Mr. Boswell stood at the room's only window and surveyed the surroundings. Below the window was a yard, mostly dirt with a struggling vegetable patch in one corner. There was an outhouse and an alley beyond it. Up and down the alley everything seemed quiet except for the occasional banging of a back door or clatter of an ash-can lid.

The detective left John Day in charge of the prisoner and ventured out to arrange their next move. He would need a wagon or buggy in order to get Kelly to the train station, and he would need to find out when the next train was leaving for Wyoming.

Omaha in the early morning hours felt safe and pleasant. He strolled along listening to the birds in the trees saluting the return of daylight. A few delivery vans rattled up and down the streets, and somewhere a sleepy voice yelled at a barking dog. Mr. Boswell smiled as he walked along. He was glad the jail had been too full to accommodate them. A nice walk among these Omaha neighborhoods was quite refreshing. His grip on the Greener shotgun relaxed a bit. He saw the clock tower of the railroad station ahead of him.

Meanwhile, back in the rooming house, scheming and evil continued to hold sway. Kelly's night's sleep had left him as refreshed as his captors. He sat on the edge of his cot with his coffee and sausage, quiet and brooding. He listened to Boswell's footsteps going down the stairs and out the front door. When he judged the detective to be out of earshot, Kane Kelly got to his feet and looked out the small window overlooking the backyard. He stood at the window quite a long time, then turned around and began beseeching John Day to allow him to visit the outhouse, as the call of nature was upon him. Compassionate and understanding, the young man agreed.

"But you'll go with the manacles on," Day told him, "and my revolver will be right up against your spine. Mr. Boswell has given me leave to shoot you if you try to make a run for it."

"Fine," said Kelly. "I don't care. Let's just go. I need to go."

The duplicitous contractor complained that his boots were under the bed and his stomach wound pained him something awful when he tried to bend over to retrieve them. As John Day bent to get the boots for him, Kelly grabbed Day's revolver from its holster and fired. The ball went deep into Day's leg, but Day proved stronger than Kelly had reckoned on. In an instant both men were on the floor grappling for possession of the weapon. Kelly had the advantage of weight and kept trying to get on top. Day was quicker and carried sinew where most men have fat, so he was able to bend Kelly's arm painfully. However, he was weakening.

Hearing the shot and the ruckus, the owner of the house dashed upstairs and into the room in time to help subdue Kelly. He summoned the boy who did the cleaning and carrying for the establishment and dispatched him to the railroad station to find Detective Boswell.

"There's shooting!" he cried as soon as he saw the detective. "Oh, you must come! Your man's been shot and that bad 'un got his gun off him!"

Mr. Boswell set off at once, setting a pace so rapid, the chore boy had to trot in order to keep up. The sight of the detective striding down the street would intimidate the dullest of men. Seeing the fire in his eyes and the determination in the way he carried the big shotgun, even stray dogs were quick to get out of his way. Horses tethered to hitch rails rolled their eyes and shied back.

Drawing near the rooming house, he saw that the front door was wide open and that the place was ominously quiet. Training and instinct kicked in. Mr. Boswell recognized how it could be a trap, the open door, the frantic boy and all. Kelly might be waiting inside with a loaded gun.

"Take cover," he told the boy. "Go on down the block and stay there."

Mr. Boswell turned and went the other

direction. To Kelly or anyone watching from the shadows of that open doorway, it would appear that he was retreating. But in actuality, he merely walked far enough to be out of sight behind the house on the corner of the block. There he broke into a run and entered the alleyway behind the boardinghouse. The front door might or might not be a trap, but he intended to go in from the rear. He stayed against the board fence that extended along the alley all the way to the boardinghouse, where there was a long gap to allow access to the yard.

His caution turned out to be fortuitous.

As he came to the end of the fence, he heard a commotion. Carefully peering around the last fence post, he saw a carriage and team standing adjacent to the outhouse, obviously part of a plot to release Kelly. Six men were crowded onto the back stoop, waving sticks and clubs and shouting for Kelly to be brought out. But blocking their way, the house owner was refusing to let them in. That stalwart old veteran had his vintage saber in one hand and a revolver in the other. None of the bullies wanted to be the first to face him.

Amid the threats and bellowing, Mr. Boswell was able to come up behind the bunch unnoticed. When he spoke there was no temerity in his tone whatsoever.

"You will not have Kelly," he stated flatly.

Detective Boswell's deep voice was calm and full of assurance. It had the effect of freezing the mob of men. They turned and saw the twin muzzles of the cocked shotgun. He pressed it against the breast of the nearest man and nobody moved or spoke.

"You work for Clifton Kelly," he said.

"Kelly said there's a bonus in it," the man said. He was the one who had been shouting the loudest for Kelly's release, but now with two loaded barrels aimed at him, he found his voice was very faint, his throat suddenly dry. "If we bring back his brother."

"That is a problem," Mr. Boswell replied. "You see, *I* have agreed to deliver his brother on a westbound train. And I will. Even if I have to cut down the six of you to do it. However . . I take you men to be working stiffs who are only trying to make a dollar and please the boss. You are not hired gunmen nor are you outlaws. Yet.

"And so I'll offer you a bonus of my own," he continued. "My bonus offer to you is this. I will let you quit these premises. I will allow you to abandon this fool idea of freeing a legally detained prisoner. I will let you leave without a load of buckshot in your body. How's that for a good bonus? Now go. Leave that carriage where it is. All of you simply walk away. Walk in the direction of the river. I'll be watching."

Like whipped dogs with tails between their legs, the half dozen hooligans did as they were told. Much later, as I was gathering my facts for the story, I happened to encounter a railroad laborer who claimed to have been one of these men.

"When I saw that shotgun," he said, "and looked into that face, all calm and full of business like that, I can tell you I was more afraid than I've ever been in all my life. I mean . . well, they was five men with me and all of a sudden the odds didn't matter a damn. I just wanted to get away and get to where I could breathe again. On the way back we ran into four more men, hunkies like us. They'd been sent to get Kelly too, or at least keep Boswell from gettin' to the train or jail or whatever. We told 'em, 'Turn around,' we said. We told 'em."

He and his comrades kept walking all the way to the rail yard without looking back. There they passed the word among the other Kelly employees that no bonus on earth would entice them to face Detective Boswell again. It was not that he was a big man, nor a particularly menacing one. But he was a determined man, a man of strength

155

with a stony self-confidence that made his opponent feel small and vulnerable. I agreed with him. I told him how I had seen Mr. Boswell silence an entire mob merely by raising his hand with two fingers extended.

Inside the boardinghouse the detective found his prisoner manacled to the heavy iron bed frame, raging and swearing great oaths of revenge. Kelly ranted and raved until he had exhausted himself, then lapsed into self-pitying sobs and offers of bribes to anyone who would release him. He screamed a while, probably hoping his rat-face brother was outside and would hear him, then lapsed into sullen silence. Mr. Boswell ignored him. John Day's wound was of more concern to him.

"How does it feel?"

"Hurts like fire," young Day said, grinning and gripping his thigh where a bandanna served to staunch the blood. "Got bitten by a horse on the leg once. This hurts almost as much as that did. Nothing broken, thank God. No bones."

"Indeed," the detective replied. The boardinghouse chore boy had returned, eager to help the famous lawman. He was dispatched to bring a doctor. He returned quickly, saying that a nearby physician was on his way.

"Good," said Mr. Boswell. "Now, young

man, I have another important mission for you, if you're willing and your employer can spare you again."

The boardinghouse proprietor nodded in assent.

"Good," said Mr. Boswell. "Do you know the police station on Sixth Street?"

The boy said he knew the place.

"Here is my card," Mr. Boswell continued. "That's the Association emblem on it, see? Go to the police station and ask for Constable Harris. If he is not there, you might find him at the jail or on patrol somewhere. A clever lad like you should have no trouble locating him in this district. When you find him, show him that card and tell him that Detective Boswell requires a dependable undercover operative. Can you remember that? An undercover operative. Tell Harris I'll meet him at the jail within the hour."

The boy was off like a shot, his freckled face red with excitement.

The detective started to speak with Mr. Ramsey, owner of the rooming house, but was interrupted by the appearance of a distinguished gentleman carrying a small black bag. The doctor was every bit as businesslike and efficient as Detective Boswell. Without any of the usual polite preliminaries, he crossed to the bed where

John Day lay and went to work on the deputy's wound. His trained fingers found the ball beneath the skin. A neat little incision with a scalpel liberated it from the flesh; alcohol was applied, which caused Day to grind his teeth in pain.

"Helps it to heal," the doctor said. "Although some say it would be better to drink it."

He followed the alcohol drench with a wrapped bandage.

"Can you walk?" Mr. Boswell asked, after the doctor had gone.

"With a stick, I'm sure I can."

Hearing this, Mr. Ramsey hurried to his own room and returned with a thick cane.

"Lodgers leave all sorts of stuff," he said, smiling.

"Thanks, Mr. Ramsey," said Mr. Boswell. "Now, what do you know about handling a team? Could you drive the carriage our visitors left behind the house, do you think?"

In reply, the veteran presented himself at attention and saluted smartly.

"Corporal Eben Ramsey," he said, "late of the First New York Artillery Brigade. Caisson driver. You heard of the battle at Cemetery Ridge?"

"Oh, yes."

"I did considerable driving *that* day, I can

tell you! I can handle your carriage all right. Where are we going?"

"We are taking Mr. Kelly to the jail. I need to get him lodged securely so I can prepare to take him on to Laramie City. His brother is out there plotting some further scheme, of that I have no doubt whatever. That evil individual has surprised me twice now, and I do not intend for him to do it again. So, if you're willing to drive, and if young Day here can suffer the journey, we'll get this bawling bully out of your establishment and behind bars."

So once again Kane Kelly, bitterly complaining about being treated so unfairly, found himself seated on the backseat of a buggy next to an officer holding a gun to his ribs. Detective Boswell rode in the front seat with his revolver drawn and ready. Corporal Eben Ramsey drove them down the alleys and among backstreets, working his way toward the town center like an army teamster sneaking up on the enemy. They were being followed and they knew it. From time to time a fence gate would slam shut, or they would hear hurrying footsteps crossing an alley behind them. Apparently Kelly's employees did not want to go back without their boss's brother. But neither did they want to risk a face-to-face confrontation with Mr. Boswell, not after seeing what it had done to the first bunch of men.

Footsteps behind them, gates being opened and shut, and then several minutes went by when they heard nothing. Not a glimpse of pursuit was to be seen to their rear. Mr. Boswell urged Ramsey to proceed slowly and to stay alert.

"They are no longer behind us," he said. "I suspect they have hurried ahead of us in hopes of laying some kind of trap."

His caution proved to be well-founded when they arrived at a spot where the alleyway crossed a street two blocks from their destination. Mr. Boswell called a halt at the entrance to the alley.

"There," he said. "This is the place. Just as I thought. They have run ahead of us and they've found their ambush site. Do you see the outhouses flanking the alley on both sides? That woodshed on the left? And there's a wooden fence. See? Almost overgrown with brush and weeds. We will wait here and watch for a few minutes."

"I don't see a soul," Corporal Ramsey said.

"Nonetheless. If I were a betting man, I would wager ten dollars that there is at least one rogue in that outhouse to starboard, and another to port. One or two are behind that fence, I'm certain of it."

It was a good setup for ambush, John Day said later. As Mr. Boswell had pointed out, on either side of the alley stood an outhouse, one with the door facing them and the other presenting a blank wall because its door faced the house. The woodshed's doorway also faced the house, but the cracks between the back wall boards would give a concealed man a clear view of the alley. Several men could also crouch behind the board fence, ready to spring out. They would probably have one man ready to seize the headstall of the off horse and hold the team while the others attacked the carriage with clubs.

"They won't dare shoot," said Mr. Boswell. "For fear of hitting Kelly. And attracting more attention."

"So what shall we do?" asked John Day.

"It's my job now," said Mr. Boswell. "My fight. You stay with Kelly and Mr. Ramsey. If they get me, I would be obliged if you would put a bullet through Kelly. If he tries to escape, shoot him. Then I'm afraid you two will need to make a run for it."

John Day saw Mr. Boswell's wink and grin, but Kelly did not see it because Kelly was staring down at the floorboards of the carriage, watching his tears making splotches in the dust.

"What do you notice about the hiding places of these miscreants, Mr. Day?"

"Notice?"

The lad sensed that Mr. Boswell intended to use the situation in order to teach him a lesson of some sort.

"Well . . we could be in a crossfire from the two outhouses. Oh, look! There's a gun barrel sticking out of a knothole. The privy on the left."

"What else?" asked Mr. Boswell as he calmly checked the loads on both his revolvers and the shotgun.

"Wood? It's all wood? Wood privies, wood fence. No brick, no stone, nothing you'd really call bulletproof. Not even thick wood, just boards."

"Good! That's what I wanted you to notice. *That* is their mistake. Their other mistake is that they cannot shoot toward Kane Kelly. And they know it. I, on the other hand, can fire in their direction freely. It's a huge advantage. I would say that we have already won the day. Don't you agree, Mr. Kelly?"

But Kelly could only sob and mumble.

"What's that you say? Speak up, man. Do you think your brother's men stand much of a chance of stopping us? They think they are hiding, but we know where they are. They think they have protection, but a pistol ball can go through those boards like they were paper."

"Let me go now!" Kelly blubbered. "If it's money, my brother will pay. My stomach hurts. I only want to get back to work. Look here, Boswell: lots of men, sixty or more, they get a paycheck from my company. Don't you see what you're doing? If you don't let me go and let me get back to running the company, all those men will be out of work. Lose their jobs. They'll be desperate for money and it'll be all your fault. What's done is done. Look, we'll pay you for your trouble, all right? Let me go now. My brother will collect me and we'll be going back into Iowa."

Detective Boswell replied by dismounting from the carriage.

"If he tries to escape," he said to John Day, "or if his men rush you, shoot him."

With the shotgun in the crook of one arm and his revolver in the other hand the detective entered the alley alone.

When Mr. Boswell narrated the incident to me some time later, I was struck by the calm, matter-of-fact voice with which he told about the strategy and dangers involved. It was almost like listening to a master woodworker describing how he selected and shaped a piece of wood, or a chess player reenacting a particularly complex game.

"Without Kelly telling me," he said, "I already knew those men were on the payroll of his contract company. No doubt his brother had threatened them with the loss of their jobs and told them all they had to do was overcome one man. Me. Then they would return to their jobs and their paychecks, and all would be well. The men who waited for us in the alleyway probably knew next to nothing about the murder of young Charlie Madalone, so I could not count on them having a sense of justice in the matter. But I have dealt with the American workingman all my career. I know they are generally honest and not given to deadly violence. Your man who works with his hands is sensible, and he thinks things through. He does not take unnecessary risks, especially the risk of injury or imprisonment. In all but a few cases they have families who are dependent upon them."

"Not to mention how poorly people would think of them if they were to end up in prison," I ventured. "Men place value on their reputations."

"Correct. And as I faced that alley ambush, I knew the attackers were out of their native element. On the open plains, beyond all touches of civilization, their toughness was their armor and they could flex it in any manner they wished. But in a large town, hiding in a householder's smelly privy or crouched behind a fence, they would feel like skulking coyotes rather than brave frontiersmen. I knew they would flee if given the chance, just as I knew they would find no shame in doing so. Running away would be the sensible thing to do. My task, therefore, was to put the fear of God into them *without* putting one of them into such a panic that he would begin to shoot — or wield a club or knife — and necessitate my shooting him down."

"Which you were prepared to do," I said.

"*If* necessary. But you must understand something, Mr. Pierce. It was taught to me by an old Oklahoma sheriff quite a few years ago. When a law officer draws his weapon and prepares to shoot at a citizen, he has already failed in his duty. If he is any good at his job, if he understands what peacekeeping is about, he should not aim a gun at a person anytime during his career. An officer's duty is to disarm and disengage; that is to say, cause the felon to drop the weapon and change his mind about resisting arrest.

Waving a loaded revolver in his face is a very uncertain way to accomplish that.

"My problem in the alley, however, was that I could not speak to the men nor reason with them. For one thing, they were not only intent upon freeing Kane Kelly in order to preserve their own salaries. Dispersed and concealed, each man no doubt felt he was somehow responsible for protecting each of the other men. I also knew, mostly by instinct and without really thinking about it, that one or two of them were bound to be trigger-happy and apt to fire at me without actually meaning to. As you know, we spotted the barrel of a gun, probably a pistol, being aimed through a knothole in the privy on the left. You'll appreciate that, should I aim *at* that privy, that firearm within would almost certainly go off. Out of fear, you see."

CHAPTER 9

"I had pointed out to John Day that our ambushers were hidden behind wooden walls. But I doubt the full significance of that fact had occurred to him. The privies, and the board fence, were several seasons old and quite dried out. The wood would be brittle."

"Ah!" I said. "So you decided to set fire to them! A few dry weeds and some trash as kindling and they would be sent scurrying."

"Mr. Pierce," the detective said, smiling, "I suggest you stick to journalism. No. For one thing, it would have been impossible to set fire to all three structures at once. For another, it would fill the alleyway with smoke and obscure both myself and the ambushers. I would not want to shoot my revolver into that smoke in the hope of hitting one of them, for a bullet might find some innocent citizen who had stepped out to see what the fire was about. And one of the assassins might shoot into the smoke toward us, possibly hitting me, Corporal Ramsey, John Day or Kane Kelly."

"I see," I said. "So fire is not the best option. Please go on."

"As I said, the wood was brittle. Now I reasoned that my first task was to flush them out into the open. Few things are more dangerous — and unpredictable — than a hiding coward with a gun. You might recall a case in Chicago last year in which a home owner became so fearful of robbery that he hid himself in his basement with food and weapons. He heard someone at the basement door, shot through the door, and killed his neighbor, who had come to see if he was all right."

"I remember that incident, yes," I said.

"The privy with the gun barrel sticking out was ahead of us and on my left. If I aimed in that direction he would surely shoot first. I therefore determined to surprise him and direct his attention away from me. When I had gotten close enough to the ambush site, I pulled the hammer of my revolver back and suddenly fired from the hip at the opposite privy, the one on the right-hand side of the alley. And this is where the dry wood comes in. When the lead ball smashed through the boards, it set off a shower of flying splinters. There was a gratifying howl of pain, and the ambusher rushed out with his face and hands bleeding from dozens of lacerations. This made the ambusher on the left withdraw his gun in order to look and see what had happened. As soon as his gun barrel disappeared, I treated him to two fast shots, again hitting the privy wall above his head and piercing his face and hands with sharp slivers. You can appreciate how terrifying it is to have your 'protection' suddenly shattered by a bullet.

"He dashed out, as I thought he might, and he dashed to join his companions hidden behind the fence. I put my fourth bullet into his leg. He yelled and swerved away, limping, losing himself among the houses. The other ambusher was also sprinting toward the fence. He had no visible weapon.

"At this point I felt I had established myself as the attacker. No doubt the rest of the ambushers had realized they could lose not only their paid jobs but their ability to perform any jobs at all should they persist in their mission.

"I holstered my revolver and advanced on the wooden fence with the shotgun. The improved model Greener proved to be an excellent weapon for this job. Not only did it punch a hole in the wooden fence, a hole the size of your head, but with both shots gone, it took only seconds to break open the breech and reload. Corporal Ramsey later remarked that the roar and smoke of the Greener reminded him of his days in the field artillery!

"In short, two shotgun blasts into the wooden fence set off another blizzard of sharp wooden splinters, and three bully boys went running up the alley. They ran for their lives, crouching and zigzagging and no doubt expecting to be struck with lead at any moment. I reloaded my revolver, returned to the carriage, advised Kane Kelly to stop his complaining and bawling, and drove to the city jail without further ado."

With his prisoner safely behind bars, Detective Boswell would have been free to wage an all-out assault on Clifton Kelly and whatever loyal followers remained. However, he was commissioned to do one thing and one thing only: to bring Kane Kelly to Laramie City and see that he stood trial for the murder of young Charlie Madalone. And so rather than go Kelly hunting, he elected to rent a room across from the jail. There he and John Day could rest and recuperate.

Mr. Ramsey could return home, proud to have helped the famed detective.

Receiving the summons from the rooming house chore boy, Constable Harris arrived. He found Mr. Boswell and Mr. Day sunning themselves on a bench outside the small hotel.

"Sorry I was delayed, Mr. Boswell," he said.

"Constable! How very good to see you again! Two years, is it? Let me introduce you to John Day, a lad of considerable courage and resourcefulness. I hope to recruit him."

"Already accomplished," said John Day grinning. "The Rocky Mountain Detective Association is just what this country needs. I'd be proud to be part of it."

"I'm glad to meet you, then," said the constable. "I would have arrived sooner, but I was sent to investigate a shooting in an alley not too far from here."

"Oh?"

"Considerable damage to a couple of privies and a board fence. Some traces of blood in one privy and elsewhere. Possibly a drunk letting off steam with his gun, or maybe a dispute between two men. We get quite a few who would rather punch each other, or shoot one another, than settle differences in a civil manner. One of them appears to have used a shotgun. A large-bore shotgun, like the one you have leaning on the bench next to you."

"You don't say," said Mr. Boswell.

"I understand you have your man," Constable Harris continued. "Kane Kelly, behind bars at last. Even this far from Laramie City, people were angered by the shooting of that boy and by Kelly's escape from justice. A few citizens recently arrived from the East wrote irate letters to the newspapers, asking how it was that a murderer could roam freely and go about his business. They don't understand the open, wild country hereabouts, of course."

"Hence the need for an association of law officers, a private association. We can be as free as the criminals, which is of great help in apprehending them."

The two friends caught up on news of one another, chatted about old times, and then Detective Boswell described his plan and asked for Harris's advice. In short, he hoped to find a man of intelligence and courage — a man such as John Day — who could be persuaded to insinuate himself into the Kelly mob and try to find out their plans. There would be a degree of risk involved, but lives might be saved.

"Kelly has sent men to ambush us, and they very nearly took me by surprise. He made an attempt at bribery. I think he's capable of anything. As I see it, he has several options. Any one of them could put the public in deadly danger. The man does not hesitate to endanger innocent citizens — indeed, he doesn't seem to consider the potential for doing so. So . . he might gather another mob of his workers to attack us between here and the railway station. He might have men on the train, waiting for us to board the cars. He might try to stop the train and seize us somewhere along the way."

"Plenty of open country between here and Laramie City," the constable agreed. "What is it, four hundred miles or more?"

"I firmly believe he is having us watched," Mr. Boswell continued. "Night and day. No doubt your visit to me is already known to his spies. If you do know of some man who might join the Kelly mob as an investigator, I will need you to approach him yourself, and with extreme discretion. On no account should he be seen speaking to me."

"As a matter of fact," the constable said, "I know of the perfect choice. Young, tough, resourceful and above all a believer in law and order. Jimmy Skroggs."

"No!" the detective said. "Not the son . . . the son of Ben Skroggs?"

"The same. And cut from the same cloth as our old comrade in arms."

"And you say he could bring off this bit of espionage?"

"I have no doubt of it. He works at the yards, you see. Apprentice to the locomotive mechanics who are teaching him the trade of steam repairman. Young Jimmy has already served me very well in a case involving an illegal distillery hidden in the repair yard, and another case of a prostitute hanging about the station. He has the advantage of looking wholly fresh and innocent, you see. But beneath that schoolboy exterior lives an extremely tough and inventive young man."

"He sounds ideal, then," said Detective Boswell. "Now if we can come up with some stratagem which will enable him to communicate with me without being seen with me. He shouldn't be seen with you, either."

"Leave this to me," said the constable. "I'll come up with a strategy. Whatever plan Clifton Kelly might have in mind, we'll soon know it."

In the days that followed it seemed as if nature herself was conspiring against N. K.

Boswell. Like Moses leading his people from Egypt, he found himself confronted with an excess of water. First it was the Missouri River, rushing over its banks because of torrential rains many miles upstream. The westbound train Mr. Boswell hoped to take to Wyoming was delayed because the railroad company had to wait for a cargo to arrive from Council Bluffs; however, the surge of high water in the Missouri made the captain of the steam ferry refuse to risk his craft in a crossing. The old river had a way of smashing floating logs and debris into boats and sinking them.

On the heels of this delay, there came a series of heavy thunderstorms, sweeping a driving curtain of torrential rain a hundred miles across, flattening the tall grass and stripping leaves from trees as it dragged across the Great Plains. The Elkhorn River west of Omaha rose to historic levels, the water ripping houses from the ground and breaking them into kindling. The Blue River became black with soil and as thick as pudding. Homesteaders up and down the Platte hurried to drive livestock to higher ground, not knowing whether their homes would still be there when they returned.

Detective Boswell became a familiar visitor at the Omaha railroad office. Each day he went to inquire about the status of westbound trains, and each day the answer was the same: no trains until crews could inspect all the trestles as far as Fort Kearney. And once the track was deemed safe, the first train had to be a string of freight cars carrying vital goods. No passengers.

"You ain't the only one frettin'," the station agent told the detective. "I'm gettin' telegraphs 'bout every day from Fort Kearney. They's somethin' real important they need . . buncha crates over there, see?"

Mr. Boswell looked. It was a sizeable consignment of wooden crates, each one stamped "US Army."

"But if they think I'm riskin' government freight on the first westbound, they're crazy. No. Them boxes have t'wait. Probably go on *your* train, whenever that is."

After each visit to the railroad office the detective would walk back to the hotel, or to the jail, telling himself to be patient. His mind, however, did not want to be patient. Maybe he could hire a wagon and team and set out for Wyoming on his own. But there would still be flooded creeks to contend with.

"Besides that," he said to Constable Harris, "I might no sooner get started than the track would be fixed and the train would leave for Laramie. And there I'd be, out on the prairie again with Kane Kelly."

And the week went by, and another long week of waiting began.

Meanwhile, Jimmy Skroggs got busy. Constable Harris's confidence in him proved to be well-placed. He had no trouble enlisting himself in the "volunteer" army of Kelly rescuers, considering that a dozen of those bullies had already chosen to resign and go back to their regular jobs rather than face the resolute Boswell again. He wanted to get out of the repair shop, Jimmy told them. Too much smoke and heat, he said. Wanted to get back to doing outdoor work on the rails.

"I heard they want to run a line north," one of the other men said. "Heard they can't get 'er started without a contractor. Onct those Kelly boys get straightened out, maybe they'll be jobs waitin' for us."

"Sure," Jimmy agreed. "Sure, the thing to do is to get Mr. Kelly free so the outfit can get back to work."

Jimmy had come up with a simple and clever strategy. At the end of day, when the conspirators usually gathered in a nearby saloon to mutter among themselves, he would simply be there. "With this innocent little face of mine," he told me later, "they sort of felt sorry for me and saw me as somebody they could recruit for their plan, whatever it was. So I got drawn into the conversation little by little, but mostly the more used they got to my being there, the more invisible I was. All I had to do was watch for a chance to help Mr. Boswell."

One evening his opportunity came.

"We need to get word to Mr. Kelly somehow," one of the leaders remarked. "Some of us got a plan, but he has t'be ready in the jail. Maybe we might pass a note through his cell window or something like that."

"Think, man!" said another. "Use your damn head, why don't you? Why, you don't even know which cell's his. What if you wrote down the plan and dropped it right into Boswell's hand?"

"Sorry?" Jimmy Skroggs said, as if he had just realized someone was speaking. "What's the problem?"

The leader turned to the new recruit like an annoyed schoolteacher.

"I was sayin' we got to let Mr. Kelly know what we're plannin', so's when it happens he'll know what to do."

"Oh. Well, I could tell him."

A half dozen dirty faces turned toward

the boy. A beer mug thumped down on the table, but otherwise everything was quiet.

"And how?" the leader said, smirking. "Just how do you think you'd be able to tell him?"

"I know the jailers. I guess I know most everybody around this part of town. I know the milk delivery man, the washerwoman over on Sixth Street — her name's Betty — and the livery man on Eighth Street, and —"

"What about the jailers?"

"When I walk home, sometimes I stop in at the jail. In the winter they're always good for a hot cup of coffee. Generally their coffee's a day old, but the building's warm. Good place to sit a while and visit, you know. I know Constable Harris, too. Sometimes when the weather's good and there's no work to do at the shops, I walk his rounds with him."

Jimmy then announced that he was going home to wash up and get some supper. He chatted on about what he hoped he would have for supper, acting as if he had forgotten why he was telling them about his strolls with the constable. But from the look on the gang leader's face, he knew that the bait had been taken.

■ ■ ■ ■

Just as Jimmy had said, his walk home took him in the direction of the police station. And who should he see loitering outside, enjoying the nice evening, but Constable Harris. Jimmy paused and made a show of pointing down the street and making hand gestures as if patting a dog. Anyone watching him from a distance, and someone probably was, would assume he was telling the constable about a stray dog he had seen. But Jimmy's words to the constable were about anything but.

"I think I've got something," Jimmy said, still petting the invisible canine. "Let's try for tomorrow evening. The Kelly bunch has some sort of scheme going, and I think they're going to trust me to tell Kelly about it. I told them I could walk into the jail and talk to him."

He laughed and made a sweeping gesture with his arm as if showing the constable how this imaginary dog had run up an alleyway.

"Tomorrow evening," he said to the constable, "get yourself into the jail without making any fuss, and find some spot where you can be hidden and overhear what I say to Kelly. You'll have to figure out how to do it. Don't let Kelly know you're there. Then I'll show up and make an excuse for seeing him, like I want to give him something from his brother, a meat pie or a jacket or something. I'll let the bunch provide me with the excuse, like it's their idea. Then I'll tell Kelly the plan his brother has in mind, and you'll overhear it."

"I like the idea," Harris said. "Then you can take a message from Kelly back to his gang, and we'll know what it is."

"Sure. And one thing — be sure Detective Boswell stays well away from the jail. They watch him all the time, and if he's anywhere near the place when I go there, they'll get suspicious."

"Don't you worry a whit," the constable said. "We'll work it on this end. It'll be slick."

Constable Harris watched Jimmy Skroggs as he went whistling on his way, pausing to pick up a pebble to toss at a battered tin can. It was a dangerous game the young man was playing, very dangerous. But like himself, and Detective Boswell, John Day and the others of the Rocky Mountain Detective Association, Jimmy accepted the risk simply because he could not do otherwise. Whether youthful recruits like Jimmy,

181

or experienced veterans like Mr. Boswell, they were men of firm ethics, men who disliked anyone committing robbery or bribery, murder or graft. It was second nature to them to stop such doings. They could not imagine living in a civilization that would tolerate any kind of criminal.

"As it turned out," Detective Boswell told me, "young Skroggs had called the hand perfectly. Kelly's mob of thugs were insecure about themselves and needed Kane Kelly's leadership, needed his approval of their ideas. So when they saw a chance to have an innocent young fellow stroll into the jail building with a package for the prisoner, and tell that prisoner their plan for his escape, they leapt at it like trout rising to a mayfly."

A package was made up carefully. It consisted of a sweater tightly folded, inside one sleeve of which they placed a note to the prisoner, a note they intended to be found by the jailers. It would indicate that an armed assault would be made on a certain night.

"That'll get 'em," Clifton Kelly sneered. "Them and that damned Boswell will have t'stay up all night on watch."

The sweater would also contain some

contraband tobacco and papers to make the ruse complete. Clifton Kelly handed it to Jimmy Skroggs.

"All right," he said. "There it is. Now here's the plan. We know Boswell's waiting for a train. But what he ain't figured on is that we'll know when it's coming. We got friends to let us know when the track's clear long before he does. Now listen, Skroggs. You tell my brother to keep on like he's doin' and not to get impatient. Soon's we know when that train's due, my boys are gonna head west along the line. Somewhere just this side of Fort Kearney there'll be a pile of ties and logs on the tracks. They'll derail the train, see? That way they can get Kane away with horses and that damn Boswell. He'll be stuck on a derailed train in the middle of nowhere. By the time he makes his way back here, we'll be long gone and back about our business. And he won't get us again, by God. Not without an army, he won't."

"So I just tell him to stick tight?"

"That's it. You tell him just t'cooperate with Boswell, and do what he says. He'll get him on a train and bring him straight to us. Then we stop the train and take him, and there *won't* be no money changin' hands, neither."

■ ■ ■ ■

With Clifton watching him from the shadows, Jimmy strolled down Sixth Street past the boardinghouse where Detective Boswell sat on the stoop with his coffee and newspaper. Jimmy merely nodded and kept on walking. At the jail he stopped a moment and appeared to be considering whether to go in or not.

From Clifton's point of view, Jimmy's ruse looked perfect. And though Clifton did not know it, Mr. Boswell's ruse was also working to perfection. The package was inspected, the "contraband" given a pass, and Jimmy was allowed to go on back to the cells and hand it through the bars. Jimmy also told Kane Kelly the intelligence concerning Clifton's plot to derail the train. Constable Harris, posing as a shabby, snoring inebriate wrapped in a ragged blanket in the next cell, took in every word.

"You're sure nobody heard?" Clifton said as he fell in beside Jimmy to walk back to the rail yard shops. His limp was still quite pronounced. "What'd my brother say?"

"It went slick as pie!" Jimmy grinned. "Went back to the cells all by my lonesome, told him everything. Nobody heard, 'cept a drunk in a cell back there. And the way he was snoring, I don't guess he was in any shape to hear anything. Your brother says he's uncomfortable as hell and wants out. He said, 'I guess I'll have to wait, but tell Clifton to get movin' on it.' And he said to be sure and bring him a gun when you take the train. That's about it."

"Well, I guess it's okay with him, then. We'll wait another day. I'll figure out what it's best for him to do and send you back. You didn't have no trouble, then?"

"No. Like I said, those boys at the jail appreciate company once in a while. They'd let me go play checkers with your brother if I asked 'em."

"Checkers," Clifton Kane snarled. "By God, we're way past playing damn checkers. This is serious business, this is. I gotta plan it slick, see? Gettin' him off the train, that's one thing I gotta plan and get it right. Gotta use surprise. Maybe we'll make it look like it's a regular railroad crew tryin' to clear the track, see? Then my boys, they'll come boilin' up outa nowhere and swarm that train. Boswell probably won't interfere. He thinks there's money for the family comin' his way."

"Sounds good," Jimmy agreed.

"Yeah, but we ain't through yet, see? You

gotta learn to think things out, you know. Next we gotta get away. Figure which way to ride, how to get across the river and all that. I gotta think of everything."

"Let me know if I can help," Jimmy said. "I gotta get back to the job now."

CHAPTER 10

Detective Boswell now knew what Clifton Kelly was planning, but he did not relax his vigilance. Other men who had gone against the law could attest to Mr. Boswell's unrelenting concentration, his unsettling patience as a lawman, his calm and methodical manner of investigation and pursuit.

The detective gradually widened the limits of his seemingly unplanned strolls through neighborhoods around the boardinghouse and jail. A typical walk would take him to the jail, then toward the rail station to see if they had heard any reports about the track repairs. He took mischievous pleasure in walking toward the shops where he might encounter Jimmy, or any one of several of Kane henchmen. These fellows would report to Clifton Kelly that he had been "snooping around," when in fact he was merely keeping the gang on edge. He would take interest in freight cars parked on the siding, peering inside the empty ones and checking the locks on those that were loaded.

One afternoon, while leaning on the freight shed doorway watching the tracks, Detective Boswell became aware of two men who were keeping him under observation. Smiling to himself, he took out a cigar and a lucifer and looked around for somewhere to sit and enjoy it. Let the Kelly boys assume he was waiting for something or someone. Keep them nervous and watchful, anyway.

Just inside the doorway of the shed he found a crate to sit on. It was one of the several boxes marked "US Army" and labeled for delivery to Fort Kearney. An idea was born.

"Tell me," he said to the stationmaster. "These crates for the army at Fort Kearney. How are they going to get there?"

"Same as you are," the stationmaster said. "Like I been tellin' you for a week, as soon as the Elkhorn River trestle is rebuilt *and* all the other bridges made safe, *and* we get a train in here, you and them crates and a bunch of other stuff will be off to points west and good riddance."

"One more thing. A woman acquaintance of mine had her things packed into a shipping crate for going back to Philadelphia.

How does that work, exactly? What I mean is, where did she get a crate, and how did she get it onto the train?"

"I know the woman you mean," the stationmaster said. "Like I told her when she asked how to ship her stuff, we've got plenty of empty crates right here, usually. A lot of people unpack their goods right at the station and then leave the crates behind. My boy found one the right size and took it to her up at the boardinghouse. She packed her things in it, then a couple of men went and got it and brought it here, and that was it. Off it went across the river to catch the next train east outa Council Bluffs."

"So it's safely gone, and so is she," Mr. Boswell stated.

"That's right," the stationmaster said. "We might be stymied for westbound trains, but so long as the ol' Missouri behaves itself, we can still send 'em east."

Detective Boswell sought out Constable Harris and gave him instructions for Jimmy Skroggs.

"Kane's brother would rather send men to do his fighting for him than do it himself. But I want to make sure he'll be on the scene next time," he said. "See if Jimmy can't convince Clifton that the thing won't

189

work unless he personally supervises it. He needs to be at the ambush."

"You're going to shoot him again?"

"Let's hope that won't be necessary. We want to set things up so that Clifton can be held responsible of the criminal acts beyond all reasonable doubt. I want him there supervising the ambush, and I want witnesses to it. I intend to arrest Clifton once and for all."

The next part of the detective's plan required some reconnaissance and a telegraph office remote enough to be safe from bribery by the Kelly Contracting Company. Supplying himself with a few days' food and a good slicker, Mr. Boswell rode west out of Omaha, out onto the open prairie, following the railroad tracks to see for himself where to expect a train-wrecking ambush. No sooner was he out of sight of the city than the wide, unpopulated plain began to assert itself as an intimidating expanse of grass, the land rising and falling again into little hollows, always covered with grass and few trees. It was a veritable desert wilderness, a Sahara with grass. Were it not for the rails of the Transcontinental Railroad and the telegraph poles punctuating the skyline, a man could be utterly lost on such a prairie.

Despite the fact that a locomotive crew would be able to see for miles down the track, there were more than enough places where an ambush could take place. Using the detective skills for which he was known, Mr. Boswell methodically catalogued these places, listing the advantages and drawbacks of each one. He kept in mind that the band of rescuers would have to come by horseback or wagon and would not want to be more than a day from Omaha. They would need a blind corner in the tracks, some place where they could set up a barrier or arrange a derailment that the train crew would not see until it was too late. And a place where the bunch could conceal themselves, some draw or hollow.

There were indications that a construction crew had been working diligently to reopen the tracks following the heavy rains and flooding. Short trestles across narrow gullies were repaired. New ballast stones had been tamped into low spots. In several places Detective Boswell could see that the crew had reinforced the rails by sliding new ties — called "sleepers" — under the steel.

Detective Boswell suddenly reined in and slapped his own forehead.

"Dunce!" he said aloud. "Horse, your rider needs a new brain! It must be time for

191

me to retire and start that little farm. Then again, maybe I'm too dumb to even raise chickens."

All of this track repair. Miles of track repair. It required carloads of ballast rock, not to mention carloads of timbers and ties. Yet with the Elkhorn River trestle compromised by the flood, no locomotive could move west out of Omaha. Which meant, of course, that an engine and work crew had come *from* the west. Of course! He had been assuming all along that the crews going out from Omaha and fixing the storm-damaged sections were the only crews. Now it was obvious that a second gang of rail workers had come *from* the west. They probably backed a locomotive and flatcars from some town — Central City, Kearney, Wahoo or Grand Island — and had fixed the washouts as they came to them.

"Horse, you know what this means, don't you? It means that somewhere along these tracks we're going to find a work camp. If it's not too far away, it could very well be just what we need. Giddup!"

In the afternoon of the second day, Detective Boswell topped another of the seemingly endless low hills of prairie grass and saw a column of smoke rising beyond the next one. He heard, then saw, a gandy car clattering along the rails, four workmen pumping at the handles. And as he rode around the next bend, his eyes widened at the welcome sight of the Union flag flying from a pole.

The camp consisted of four Union Pacific tents with the "U.P." initials stenciled on the canvas and four additional tents of the US Army. Behind the tents he could see a neatly arranged line of wagons and a rope corral of horses. Parked on a newly built railroad siding was a locomotive and two flatcars. One of the features most welcome to the detective's eyes was a small tent near the siding, a tent from which two wires led up an adjoining telegraph pole.

Within minutes his horse was being cared for by a soldier who was glad for something to do. Detective Boswell was in one of the U.P. tents where he was offered a chair and a mug of tea. He accepted both with thanks. His host introduced himself as the supervisor of the work camp.

"Your reputation comes ahead of you, Mr. Boswell," Mr. Thomas Ring said with a smile. "Based in Laramie City, you see. Heard of your campaign against the criminal class, and we stand behind you all the way. May I introduce this young gentleman in blue? Lieutenant William Wheeler, commander of a squad of infantry. Assigned to protect our work camp from predatory Indians. Fortunately, there have been no predatory Indians."

The conversation ran to what the weather was doing, and the condition of the tracks, and the general news about Omaha and Council Bluffs.

"Hoping to find myself relocated to Omaha soon," Mr. Ring said. "Strictly confidential, mind you. Engineers have finished drawing up plans for a trestle bridge. Very long, very ambitious trestle bridge. When finished, it will span the Missouri at Omaha. Told I'm high on the list of supervisors to start the work."

"It will come as bad news for the ferry operators," said Mr. Boswell, "this bridge across the river. But inevitable. It's a tedious process, the ferrying of trains. On the day I left, in fact, they were preparing to haul an engine over from Council Bluffs, along with a string of freight cars. But the river is still running high."

"And what brings you out here to the middle of the Nebraska prairie?" Lieutenant Wheeler asked.

"I hope to prepare an ambush for some ambushers," said the detective. "It's about this Kane Kelly business."

He saw the color rise in the lieutenant's face.

"Damn that man!" he said. "Plain cowardly murder of that young lad. And then to break jail and walk away! The whole thing stinks to heaven."

"Worse yet," Mr. Ring added. "Scuttlebutt has him contracting again. That line being built in Iowa. South of Red Oak."

"Unbelievable," Lieutenant Wheeler said. "You mean to say the government and the railroad company are still paying that scoundrel when he ought to be in prison?"

"Not working for our U.P., I'm glad to say," Mr. Ring said. "Different line entirely. Offensive to civilized people anyway. Pleased to learn that the Rocky Mountain Detective Association had been called in to bring Kelly to justice, very pleased."

"Let me bring you gentlemen up to date, if you will allow me."

Detective Boswell narrated the sequence of events from his being engaged by the Madalone family to the recent incarceration of Kelly, who currently was awaiting transport to Laramie City.

"Excellent news!" Mr. Ring said. "Proud to say my crew fixed the tracks to carry Kelly to the gallows! Excellent."

"There are complications, however," said Detective Boswell. He explained how Clifton Kelly had made several ill-advised but serious attempts to set his brother free.

"Clifton is a cowardly sort, like many bullies," the detective told them. "He's very good at stirring up a mob to do his dirty work. He uses bribery and the threat of unemployment to keep men in line, but so far he has done nothing he could be arrested for. There would be no evidence against him. But he has become a thorn in my side, so to speak, and I intend to see him behind bars before Kane Kelly's trial begins. I do not want Clifton Kelly free to start a courtroom riot. Or worse."

"How can we help?"

"I'm glad you asked. That's why I am here."

Mr. Boswell outlined Clifton's latest scheme, the plot uncovered by young Jimmy Skroggs, which was to lie in wait for the train somewhere west of Omaha, derail the cars, then free the prisoner by force.

"Clifton believes that he has bribed me into cooperating with this plan. I'm supposed to think there will be a mock assault, some kind of ambush or derailment to stop the train. Then a quick skirmish, I surrender, I release his brother, and the Kellys ride away. He promises a great deal of money to be handed over for Charlie Madalone's family, but of course that won't happen."

"But he doesn't need to derail the train, does he?"

"Oh, yes. Clifton is single-minded, like a rat chewing his way into a pie cupboard. All he can see is his brother and him escaping over the prairie. But he's a cautious rat. He will not leave any way for me to pursue him or go back to Omaha for assistance. He needs to leave me stranded, even if it means derailing a train. Or having his thugs do it, in order to keep his own hands clean."

"And how will you meet such an attack?" asked Lieutenant Wheeler. "I imagine they plan to block the track with some kind of barrier, possibly remove a rail. Then order everyone off at gunpoint."

"Friends of mine in Omaha are making the arrangements to foil Kelly's plot. The idea is to have a posse, a number of armed volunteers, riding in an open train car ahead of the locomotive. We may push several cars, in case the ambushers do try a derailment. The posse concealed in the open car could stave off Kelly's crew and give me time to arrest Clifton."

"What if he doesn't actually participate?"

"I have another scheme going, a plan to draw Clifton to the scene of the ambush. A large piece of cheese, you might say, to make him appear in person, where I hope to arrest him."

"On what charges?" asked the lieutenant.

"Very serious charges, if my plan succeeds. Our westbound train will be carrying a consignment of crates addressed to the US Army at Fort Kearney, along with various sacks of mail. This gives me the opportunity to arrest Clifton Kelly for sabotage. For interfering with government mail. For attempting to prevent shipment of military goods. And for attempting to free a legal prisoner of a licensed law officer. Serious charges, charges from which he cannot walk away. If all goes as I hope it will, I expect him to face trial by the federal government. After which he will become a guest in the new penitentiary they recently finished building in Lincoln."

Before leaving the construction camp, the detective gathered all the intelligence he could. He found that Mr. Ring's work crew was employed by a contractor out of Cheyenne, and none of those men had anything good to say about the Kelly outfit. Kelly's men were believed to be troublesome, lazy and undependable. Ring's crew would stand with him against any number of Kelly men.

Mr. Boswell also found out that the telegraph operator at the construction camp was on a first-name basis with at least two other members of the Rocky Mountain Detective Association. He spoke despairingly of his counterpart in Omaha, a telegrapher known to be in cahoots with the Kellys and known to have exchanged confidential information for cash. This could not be proven, of course, but certain "coincidences" concerning railroad contracts seemed very suspicious.

"You let me know how I can help," he said.

The soldiers were also going to be invaluable in Detective Boswell's plan to arrest Clifton Kelly. Lieutenant Wheeler was quick to admit that his men were bored. They had little to do all day except graze the horses and patrol the hills. Several had asked if they could take off their uniforms and do some hard labor on the rails, just for the change.

"Two of my lads are experienced scouts," the lieutenant told Mr. Boswell. "They might prove useful to you."

Early the following morning Mr. Boswell took breakfast with the foreman, the lieutenant and the telegrapher.

"I need to be getting back to Omaha," he said. "Thank you for your offer of co-operation. If we should prove successful, we will rid the railroad — and the western movement in general — of two highly undesirable gentlemen. I made some notes last night, which I will share with you. And, of course, your opinions and suggestions will be welcome.

"First, here is a page from my notebook on which I have listed some code words. The Association has used them in other operations in order to mislead criminals who might have access to the telegraph lines. Most of the code words are simple negation: for instance, as you can see here on the sheet, if I wire you that *all is quiet, stop, stand down, stop,* it actually means that the train with Kane Kelly and me is on its way west and for everyone to be on the alert. While we are speaking of telegraph, can you supply a soldier with a portable key and instruct him how to use it?"

"Nothing easier," said the telegraph operator.

"Perhaps your two restless young scouts would like to reconnoiter eastward? Should they happen to spy out some unfamiliar gandy dancers working on the rails, they could send a coded message back to you?"

"Good!" said the lieutenant. "They are clever lads, these two. I'm sure they can locate the ambush and get word to me."

"And then when you get my message that our train has started from Omaha, you could prepare to surprise the ambush party."

"Exactly," Wheeler replied.

Mr. Ring was not to be left out of this promised bit of excitement.

"My boys will be eager and keen!" he said. "They won't let the army have all the fun! Track breakers and train wreckers are something they especially detest. You send the word, Mr. Boswell, and you'll see our engine coming to you. Pushing a flatcar full of men. I'm thinking we might take railroad ties and build a kind of breastwork on the flatcar. My men are in excellent condition, and they'll be in a fighting mood if they see their tracks being wrecked! If Kelly's boys want to waltz with us, by God we'll waltz with *them*!"

"I've no doubt of that." The detective smiled. "Remember that it's Clifton Kelly I want, and I want him caught red-handed. He's thin, about your height, has a thin face and sharp nose. Oh, and he walks with a limp."

"I'll let the men know. And that you want to catch him in the act, so to speak."

"Right," Detective Boswell said. "In the act."

Omaha City slept peacefully in the faint light of first dawn. Wisps of mist rose off the river to drift among the town's five hills, and all was as quiet as fog. Down at the rail yard an engineer and his fireman had left their beds while it was still dark and were getting the steam up and loading wood and water into the tender of their locomotive.

"I see your voyage across the Missouri went without mishap," Detective Boswell was saying to them. The locomotive they were working on was the one that had been ferried across the unpredictable river by barge.

"One narrow miss by a floating sawyer," the engineer said. "Big tree log in the water. Big long roots turnin' over and over, comin' at us. But everything went smooth as silk otherwise. She is a beauty, ain't she?"

The crew's pride in their locomotive was fully justified. The boiler and cab gleamed with shiny black paint, generously decorated with fanciful scrollwork in chrome and brass. Every bit of metal was new and shining, from the cowcatcher up to the brass whistle. But as if it could never be shiny enough to suit him, the engineer kept on polishing drive rods and connecting arms with his rag while he chatted with Detective Boswell.

"So you say there's some plot afoot that could wreck my engine?" he asked.

"Have you heard of the Kelly contractors?"

"Oh, not *them* boys!" The engineer spat on the ground. "Why, an engine driver was killed last month 'cause of them, down on the southern line in Iowa. Kelly skimped on the ballast for a big curve and it gave way. Dumped th' engine, tender and all. Can't prove Kelly did it, but everybody knows. Criminal, that's what it is. Criminal."

"And criminal is precisely why I am in Omaha," Mr. Boswell said. "I can see the both of you gentlemen are honest and of good character, no doubt have good families and are regular church members."

"I see why they say you're a good detective!" the fireman said. "Two fine children and a loving wife here, a good Presbyterian. Sorry to say it, but my engineer is Methodist. And a family man. Now, what were your clues?"

"Never mind that," Mr. Boswell said. "I am about to ask you to engage with me in a little legal subterfuge, a kind of necessary deception, if you will. It may result in you finding yourselves held at gunpoint, but I have every confidence that your lives will not be endangered. No doubt you've been apprised of the fact that the westbound tracks will soon be open. I have Mr. Kane Kelly in my custody, accused of murder. I intend to deliver him to the marshal at Laramie City."

"We'll get you through, Detective! Why, those four hundred miles will whiz by when you're ridin' behind this beauty."

"No doubt," the detective said. "However, I've learned that Mr. Clifton Kelly plans to stop this train and retrieve his brother, even if it means wrecking the engine. I have already faced his bully crew and found them quite cowardly when all the chips were down. But this is Clifton's final opportunity to free his brother, and he may whip his men into desperate frenzy in order to carry it off."

The engineer had a gleam in his eye.

"We're with you, Detective!" He looked to his fireman, who nodded in agreement. "As for the danger, nuts! Why, don't we spend our days crossing all that godforsaken empty prairie where we could get derailed by buffalo or Indians or washouts at any minute? At fifty miles per hour, Mr. Boswell, hazards can come at us before we know it.

And there's the fire and boiler. Look at this cab. Look how narrow she is, and right between a pile of firewood and a blazing firebox, with a giant tank of steam right at eye level not six feet from our faces. Risk? Mr. Boswell, it don't get much riskier. So you bring on Mr. Kelly and his hunkies, and we'll see what they're made of."

In complete confidence that he could trust these fine men, Detective Boswell told them all the details of Kelly's plan and of his own. He suggested they concoct a story for the benefit of the rail yard workers that a flatcar should be loaded with heavy railroad ties, the loaded flatcar to be pushed ahead of the engine as far as Fort Kearney. By this means, it would be the flatcar that would hit any weak rails or shaky trestles, not the engine. In fact, the flatcar could be uncoupled and pushed ahead manually to test any danger spots.

Word of this flatcar arrangement spread until one of Clifton Kelly's spies heard of it, whereupon it was soon relayed to Clifton Kelly. But it did not change his plans a whit. When his boys pulled the spikes, whether they derailed the engine or the flatcar, it wouldn't matter. The train would be stopped. Clifton figured that Boswell would not resist because he was going to get all that money "for the family." They would grab Kane from the passenger car and be off on horseback and wagons onto the trackless plains. Some of his men would disable the engine, if it was still on the rails, so by the time Boswell got back to Omaha, the Kelly brothers would be long gone. It was a perfect plan.

Detective Boswell had a plan of his own. He left the engineer and fireman to their work and went to visit the freight office. The box he wanted was still in the lumber shed, a large wooden crate stenciled with US ARMY PROPERTY in black letters.

"That there had an artillery limber in it. For Fort Dodge," the freight agent explained. "A sergeant and couple of blue boys came an' unpacked her, put the wheels on and hitched a pair of mules, drove her right off the platform. Left the crate behind. So you want it?"

"Indeed," said Mr. Boswell. "Indeed I do. Could some of your boys load it on a wagon and bring it to the hotel, and then retrieve it when it's loaded?"

"That's what we do," the agent said with a sniff. " 'Course we could."

"Today, then. Bring it to the hotel today. I want to make that train when it leaves, and

I want that crate to be in one of the boxcars."

"She'll be there," the agent said. "You fill
'er, we'll ship 'er! I'll write it down on the
manifest right now."

Mr. Boswell ate his noon supper at the
Front Street Saloon and Grill and walked
back to the hotel. The owner was cleaning
some lamp chimneys at a table in the front
parlor.

"I'll wager that you have a stack of surplus
mattresses somewhere," Mr. Boswell said.

"Why, you're right!" the hotel owner said.
"A big pile in a spare room. Can't put 'em
in the basement — rats and mold, you
know. I get new ones, at least a few every
season. Old ones get stained, you know, or
get lumpy. I'd sure like to get rid of the old
ones, but there's no way. Short of paying to
have 'em hauled, that is. Well, I could do it,
but just ain't had the time."

"They'll be bringing a big crate up from
the railroad station this afternoon," Mr.
Boswell said. "I would like to purchase some
mattresses to pad the inside of it for a
somewhat fragile cargo. Do think you could
do that for me? And could you do it before
nightfall? My idea is to have a narrow mat-
tress on the bottom, one on either side, one

on the top, something to pad either end. Leaving a cavity approximately large enough for a man to lie down in."

"Certainly, sir!" the hotel owner said. "I've got just the boy for the job, clever with wire and laths and such. He'll build you as cozy a compartment as you could want."

"Excellent," said the detective. "That will be excellent!"

And he walked toward the jail, whistling a little tune.

As it happened, I turned into Sixth Street in time to see that familiar figure ahead of me. The strong, square shoulders, the head held erect, and the purposeful stride could be those of no other man.

"Detective Boswell!" I called.

He turned and saw who had called his name.

"Why, it's Mr. Pierce again!" he said.

His handshake was strong and warm. I couldn't stop grinning. Standing before Mr. Boswell made me feel as though my life had been floating in limbo up until now, and now it had some direction and meaning again. I cannot explain the feeling better than that.

"Still with the newspaper?" he said.

"Indeed," I said. "I heard you had Kane

Kelly in the Omaha jail. I'm hoping to interview him for a story. Both the *Daily Herald* and the Cheyenne *Leader* are interested."

"Walk along with me, then," he said. "For I'm on my way to check on him. His wound has healed well enough — your newspaper account of how he came to be wounded was quite accurate, by the way, and I much appreciate that you did not call it a 'lucky' shot — but his customary mood is one of gloom punctuated by moments of rage. The man seems certain, absolutely certain, that one of these days he will return to his contracting job as if nothing happened. It's almost beyond credibility."

"Tell me," I said. "I can't help being curious. Why would you not want me to say it was a lucky shot? Perhaps it was."

Detective Boswell smiled and clapped me on the shoulder.

"I told you that a law officer should never need to draw his weapon. A villain facing a determined officer who will not draw is thrown off, loses some of his confidence wondering what that officer will do rather than pull a gun on him. It serves much the same purpose for a lawman to be known as a crack shot. Perhaps he is just lucky, but the reputation for never missing his target also makes a villain think twice."

"I see. And so what are your plans for Kane Kelly?" I asked.

He stopped and turned to me. I felt those clear eyes sizing me up again. He was trying to decide how much information a reporter can be trusted with.

"The plan," he said, "is to return him to Laramie City for trial. That is what the contract with the Rocky Mountain Detective Association calls for, and that is what I shall do."

"His brother is still at large, I assume. Will he be a problem?"

"Clifton *is* at large, principally because no charge can be laid against him. I am convinced he instigated that trouble back in Iowa, but every witness who could attest to his involvement is also an employee of the Kelly Contracting Company. The woman he paid to bribe me has gone to Philadelphia, so she cannot be a witness. As to whether he will be a 'problem,' as you put it, I would say he is likely to provide some excitement. It's over four hundred miles of open country to Laramie City. Anything could happen."

"Do you think he has a scheme in mind, some way to set his brother free?"

"I am certain of it. In fact — and I speak

210

in confidence now, and not for any ears but yours — I am reasonably sure that I know what his plan *is* and how to thwart it. The trick, however, will be to lure him into doing something illegal in front of reliable witnesses. It is Clifton's custom to send hired men to do his work for him. They have beaten up rivals, intimidated railroad agents, sabotaged tracks and equipment in order to provide more work for the Kelly Contracting Company. If they think they can get away with it, Kelly's boys even threaten their own men with exposure and arrest, you see. If the thugs get caught, they are bailed out and find themselves in debt to the Kellys for it. And you know right well that if there's one thing an American hates, it's being beholden to someone. If I can get Clifton Kelly locked up for a few years, those men should take it as an opportunity to resettle in places far away. The organization will fall apart. I have not had dealings with Sligo Kelly, the third brother, but from what I've seen of him, I don't believe he could run the company."

"It's a shame I can't put all of this in my story," I said.

"Indeed. However, Mr. Pierce . . ."

"Yes?"

"Perhaps you'd like to come along on the

211

excursion to Laramie City? If you have the time, that is. And before you say yes or no, I must confess my motive. I would like to have a newspaperman along as a witness. I would expect you to help expose the Kelly operation, and I would depend upon your — shall we say restraint? — in describing details of the Rocky Mountain Detective Association. We prefer as much anonymity as possible. You understand."

As I said, being in the presence of Detective Boswell seemed somehow to start life's vital fluids flowing again. His offer to let me share his next venture made those fluids rush through my brain, made my very muscles swell. *This* was what being a newspaper writer was about.

"I'd be thrilled," I blurted. "Thrilled! And you can be sure that I'll show you every bit of news copy before I send it in."

"Done, then," he said. "I can't say for certain when we will be leaving Omaha, but I can tell you the determining factors. First, the railway office needs to announce that the tracks are safely repaired. And of course they will need to ascertain that there will be full water tanks and wood supplies all along the route. Secondly, my informants — and possibly yours — will notice that Kelly's men are no longer to be found loitering around the Omaha saloons and railroad yard. I believe they will acquire wagons and horses and head west onto the open plains in order to set up an ambush for the train. So, when we hear that the track is ready and the Kelly boys are on their way out of town, we will arrange our train and make a start. If you keep your eye on the railway station you will see when things are ready."

"I'll sleep in a freight car if I need to," I said. "You won't leave without me!"

"Funny you should say you would sleep in the freight car," the detective said with a smile, "among the boxes and crates. What a coincidence."

CHAPTER 11

The railway station became my first regular stop as I made my daily prowl about town for stories. And if *I* was eager to see the train start out for Wyoming, the crew was downright anxious. They fretted over the engine as if it were their entry in a beautiful-baby contest. Brass work was polished daily, the black paint likewise. Pistons and connecting rods were cleaned repeatedly and fresh oil applied. The water tank was kept brimming and the billets of wood in the wood tender were arranged and rearranged in neat patterns.

Following Detective Boswell's suggestion, the crew put a flatcar in front of the engine and saw that it was loaded with railroad ties. It would serve to test any suspicious-looking sections of track and would be an effective battering ram should the Kelly crew decide to erect a barricade across the tracks. The engineer came up with a joke, and was so proud of his wit that he repeated it to everyone who came near the train. Pointing at the load of heavy railroad ties, which were often known as "sleepers," he would say, "Generally we have sleepers in the passenger cars behind, but this trip we're pushin' 'em up front!"

Immediately following the engine and tender came a boxcar modified for the postal service. The front half had been made into a cozy compartment complete with its own small stove and windows. There was a little desk where the mail clerk could sort the mail and write in his ledgers, and a folding cot for sleeping. Cubby holes and shelves held the various mail sacks. One drawback, however, was that the mail clerk had to enter and leave his mail room through the boxcar, as the only door was the one in the bulkhead.

Next in line were three passenger cars.

"I imagine there's a crowd of people who've been waiting to travel west," I said to the engineer.

"Enough," he said. "The really anxious ones went ahead by coach, though. Mostly they took a stage to one of the Nebraska stops on th' other side of the flood area. Picked up a train there. We'll have two cars. They'll be full of passengers. Mr. Boswell's party will take up most of the third one."

Two more boxcars were hitched on behind the passenger cars, and the train was complete. Freight seemed to materialize out of nowhere to fill the boxcars. One day I would see a car standing almost empty, and the next day it would be halfway filled with crates and boxes. But Mr. Boswell's padded crate was not among them.

"We're savin' room for it," the freight agent told me when I asked. "Y'see, there's a real art to packin' a boxcar. Y'need to know what's comin' and what y'got. Gotta balance the weight over the wheels or else the car might pitch back and forth, and o' course y'gotta balance 'er port to starboard, or else she'll fall over on the curves. Heavy stuff on the bottom, lighter stuff higher up."

"I guess I'd never thought of it," I confessed.

"Oh, yeah. She's an art all right. Now Mr. Boswell had me come look at that there crate of his an' I got a place saved for it. On the floor of th' first boxcar, dead center. Y'know, I asked what was in it and he said 'oh, nuthin' particular,' but I got me a theory."

His voice dropped to a conspiratorial whisper, so I leaned in closer and looked interested.

"A coffin," he said. "I'm bettin' he's ordered a mahogany coffin. He told Mrs. Harris up to the hotel one day he wished the kid at Fort Steele had a proper mahogany coffin and decent burial. That kid who got killed by Kane. Why else would anybody put padding in a big crate like that, 'cept to ship somethin' like a pianoforte or a polished mahogany coffin?"

Why else indeed?

Mr. Boswell's assessment of the rail yard situation proved to be correct. News that the track was repaired came across the telegraph lines. That very same day, men known to be in the employ of Clifton Kelly were seen leaving town with wagons and an assortment of horses and mules. I stopped at the hotel where Detective Boswell took his lunch, but was told to look for him at the telegraph office. And there he was, lounging in a chair and reading a telegram.

"More news about the track?" I said.

"No," he said. "I sent a code message to the army telegraph post so they will be expecting us. I should have a reply soon. This particular telegram is from Mrs. Elisabeth Greene, saying that she hopes I am well and that my mission was successful."

"Oh," I said. "The attractive widow. And

how did she know to telegraph you in Omaha?"

"Perhaps she's a shrewd detective. Smart as well as attractive. Or perhaps it was in answer to a telegram I sent her. To discover whether she had arrived safely, you know."

"I see," I said.

It would not have surprised me to learn that the detective and the Colonel's widow had discovered a mutual attraction. I was pondering how to broach the question diplomatically when my thoughts were interrupted by a shout from the telegraph operator.

"Here it is!" he said. His key clattered into life.

"Indian activity north. Stop. Rails clear. Stop. Not expecting large force. Stop. Ready to receive freight. Stop."

"And what does it mean?" I asked.

"As Shakespeare's King Henry says, our game is afoot! The battle is about to begin. Lieutenant Wheeler's message means his scouts are watching a small party of men — 'Indian activity north' — preparing to derail the train. 'Rails clear' means the sabotage is underway. 'Not expecting' means he has learned that Kelly has a bunch of men coming his way. And I take his last phrase to mean he is ready for us to come."

Detective Boswell summoned the telegraph operator's boy. He handed him a coin and a list of names.

"Quick as you can," he instructed the boy, "run and find these men. Begin your search at the hotel, then the café, then the livery and so forth. You are to tell them I've bought their tickets. Say nothing more, only that phrase. 'Mr. Boswell has bought your ticket,' that's all. Understand?"

The lad nodded and was off like a shot.

Following the detective's orders I was at the rail yard by six the next morning. With a full head of steam, the engine puffed impatiently and seemed to complain about being held in check each time it blew off unused steam pressure. Three men in coveralls were loading the large padded crate. The freight agent was right; the crate was the right size to hold a coffin, or perhaps a harpsichord or pianoforte. The three workmen made sure it was secure in the center of the car, then slid the door shut and locked it. Mr. Boswell turned from supervising this operation and smiled to see me.

"Ah, Mr. Pierce! Good of you to join us. Come, we'll find seats in the forward car."

We went up the steps and into the passenger car. As we made our way up the aisle,

Mr. Boswell introduced the eight men who would accompany us. They were volunteers from town, he said, and would ride along at least as far as the ambush. In their dark coats and large-brimmed hats, they looked like a posse of detectives, although I recognized a couple of them as local merchants. Each man was armed with at least one pistol that I could see. Two had Henry repeating rifles with them.

"I don't see Constable Harris or Jimmy Skroggs," I said. "Nor do I see your prisoner. Kelly? Where is he?"

"Harris and Skroggs are riding with the engineer and fireman," the detective told me. "I asked them to suffer the discomfort of riding in the wood tender where they could protect the engine and its crew. I doubt that Clifton and his men would resort to harming the engineer by shooting at him or sabotaging the engine, but I won't take the chance."

"And Kane Kelly? Where is he?"

"You'll find out. In due time."

We seated ourselves, and Detective Boswell waved his arm out the window. This was the signal to the freight agent on the platform, who relayed it to the engineer. With a heavy exhalation of steam and a jerk of the couplings, we began to move out of the station. In a few minutes we would be rolling at high speed out of Omaha, away from any sight of towns, into the open and virtually uninhabited broad prairie. The two deputies riding in the tender and every man in the forward passenger car of that moving train knew full well that we could be heading into a rendezvous with anarchy and violence. Before us lay an empty, indifferent land in which the only law was five cartridges in a revolver, the only justice was the sixth one under the hammer.

"I'm still curious about Kane Kelly," I said.

"Are you sure you would recognize him?" The detective had a bit of sparkle in his eye and a playful smile on his lips.

I looked around at the other men in the passenger car. With their broad hats and dark coats, they did look remarkably alike. I had to confess that if Kelly had been one of them, I could have missed it. As I said, I did recognize two of them while the others seemed to be strangers.

"I see your point," I said. "But now that I *am* looking for him, I'm sure he isn't in this car."

"Correct," said Mr. Boswell.

"Then where is he?"

"You reporters," Mr. Boswell said, smiling. "Always eager to find the facts. Very . . what's the term for it . . single-minded?"

"Part of the job," I said.

The train had now picked up speed and was going along with that familiar relaxing sway. Mr. Boswell continued the conversation.

"Rather than dwell on facts," he said, "why don't we pass the time with a little game of speculation. Pretend, for instance, that you are one of Clifton Kelly's gang. You're probably a pick-and-shovel man. Maybe you're a tie hack who rose to foreman, helps build trestles and so on. But you're not a road agent or criminal. Chances are you don't even own a gun. Kelly has brought you out here on a wagon. He has explained that you and your colleagues are going to stop the westbound train. This is not exactly in your line of work, but you are on the Kelly payroll, and so you have to go along with it."

"I'm with you so far," I said.

"Now let's assume that you and the other workmen have succeeded in stopping the train. You loosened a section of rail, built a barricade across the tracks, something like that. Kelly now expects you to board the cars and find his brother Kane and get him off of the train. As for himself, he is going to remain in hiding while you and the boys do the job."

"All right."

"Keep trying to put yourself in the foreman's mind. You are nervous. You've been told to confront a group of men who may have concealed weapons. Somewhere on the train is a detective who has already shot both of the Kelly brothers. You come up into this car, the one in which we are sitting, and you realize that you don't really know how to recognize Kane Kelly. What do you do next?"

I tried to imagine myself in the role of a nervous workman turned train bandit.

"Let me see," I said. "I might have a pistol with me. However, I could not be certain of disarming this many men, what with the chance of hidden pistols and all. I would need to set another man to guard all of you while I searched elsewhere, or I would get one of the other men to do the search. To search the whole train."

"Beginning with the other passenger cars," he suggested.

"Yes. And there again I'd need at least one dependable man in each car to watch the passengers. Your western traveler tends to go well armed and is not usually the type to be cowed by a bandit. A car full of armed citizens could endanger my entire project."

"And so now you are becoming even more nervous," the detective suggested.

"Oh, yes, most certainly," I said. "Now let me assess my situation. I'm some kind of boss, right? Clifton has put me in charge. So let's see. I need to have two men positioned at the engine, where they are in a standoff with Harris and Skroggs. There will have to be one or two men standing guard over you and your posse in this car. I need one or two in each of the other cars in case some passenger decides to be a hero. There would also need to be some men on the ground, on either side of the train."

I stopped as a realization struck me.

"Do you know what?" I said. "I have my forces spread out to where I cannot effectively communicate with them."

"Very good. You have made a very plausible assessment indeed. The enemy is spread out, and out of touch with one another. Perhaps you should give over the newspaper business and become a military officer. Now, just for the sake of conversation, why don't you drop the role of the foreman and pretend you are Clifton Kelly instead. And let's say that your stooge has failed to recognize Kane Kelly among the people on the train. He reports that he cannot find your brother in the passenger cars. What do you do next?"

"It's time to search the cars myself. Yes. The whole thing is taking too long. I would have to look for him myself. In the passenger cars and in the freight cars. I might think you had hidden him in a boxcar, guarded by one of your deputies."

"So you order your men to begin breaking into the freight cars. You're now officially guilty of train robbing, in front of witnesses. Now, Mr. Train Robber Kelly, imagine that one of your boys comes running toward you with the intelligence that some army troops have been spotted riding over the distant hill. In less than half an hour they will be upon you."

"Panic!" I said. "No, wait. I still have a chance to find my brother."

This game of playacting was quite intriguing. I found myself actually thinking I was in the role of Clifton Kelly.

"Aha!" I exclaimed. "I have heard about your mystery crate! The one padded with mattresses! My spies in Omaha found out about it! I need to find that crate, and quickly, for he may be in it. But I'm still not certain that he isn't in the passenger cars. My men are scattered around the train. Most have never seen my brother and don't know what Kane even looks like. They are a bunch of inept, blundering spike-strikers and hunkies. We are in danger of capture! I must do it myself. Clearly, I must find Kane myself if it is to be done."

"Perhaps you need to go into acting, Mr. Pierce. You're quite the dramatist. And so? What next?"

"I hurry through the passenger cars to be certain he is not there. Not finding him, I leap up into the nearest freight car and begin trying to open any large crate I come to. I find one crate — the one my spies described — and I call for some kind of tool to rip it open. There is more delay while one of my men finds a pick or hammer. Finally I get the crate open."

"And what do you discover?"

"Kane, my brother. Lying on the mattresses. But he is bound and gagged, which will delay things even more while I release him."

"Good idea," said Detective Boswell, "but incorrect. You'll find an empty box. He's not there. Now your frustration is on the verge of panic. What do you do, in your state of mind?"

"I don't know," I confessed. "My hoodlums and I have searched everywhere . . . no! No, we have not looked everywhere. We have not looked into the locked mail room in the forward baggage car. Aha! We proceed to the mail room, break in, probably find Kane tied up in there, and we still have time to escape. So . . am I right, Detective? Have you hidden Kane Kelly in the postal car?"

Detective Boswell laughed. Apparently he found my theatrical interpretation of Clifton Kelly quite amusing.

"Very good," he said. "Now, allow me to now sum up your situation from the point of view of a law officer. You, Clifton Kelly, are now guilty, with many witnesses, of attempted train wrecking and endangerment of passengers on a transcontinental railroad. This is a federal offense. You have committed kidnapping and assault with deadly intent and with deadly weapons. You have interfered with a licensed officer in charge of a prisoner. You have broken into secured private property and caused damage. And now, Mr. Kelly, *now* you tell me that you are prepared to break into the United States mail and use a deadly weapon to threaten a postal employee."

The detective opened his penknife and began to scrape out the bowl of his pipe.

"No," he smiled, "you will not be returning to your contracting business any time soon, unless the federal penitentiary happens to need a railroad built within its walls. You might get a job working as a common laborer on the new territorial prison being planned for Laramie."

I sank back in my seat.

"Mr. Boswell," I said, "I take my hat off to you. Remind me never to play chess with you. Or poker. He is a dangerous rat, but you have prepared an excellent trap for him."

"And there is one more surprise in our gift basket," he said, "one more trick to try on our train robbers. You may find it quite amusing, quite interesting."

"You haven't disappointed me so far," I said. "Please. Tell me."

"Jimmy Skroggs, that inestimably resourceful young man, learned that the freight shipment on this train includes a crate of replacement rifles destined for the Eighteenth Infantry at Fort Casper. Brand-new Springfield fifty-sevens. With my approval, Jimmy spread this information among Kelly's men. The crate of guns is portable and very valuable; thus, it presents an almost irresistible temptation to the rogues. If any of Clifton's men interrupt the search for Kane Kelly in order to seize upon that shipment of rifles, they will instantly become the target of an army indictment.

Another federal offense, you see."

"But if they start *using* those rifles . . . ," I said.

"No ammunition," Mr. Boswell said.

The train sped on through the morning's crystalline air. I opened the window and watched the smoke from the locomotive streaming back, listened to the steady click, click, click of the wheels on the rails, inhaled the elusive incense of burning pine wood. While I knew full well that there were small towns ahead of us, pockets of civilization with houses and streets huddled together around some water source or some intersection of trails, I could not banish the sensation that the train was carrying us into an endless waste of grass and brush where tremendous herds of bison and ancient Indian warriors sat on their ponies watching in curiosity as our frail machine went scurrying past. Our only contact with our own world consisted of two thin strips of steel laid on wooden timbers. One or two spikes missing, or a log across the tracks, and we would find ourselves stranded and at the mercy of the Great Plains.

We crossed the low trestle at Coal Creek without a tremor, then the bridge over Turtle and Raccoon Creeks, Swede's Slough and Rock Creek.

"Coming up on the Elkhorn," one of the men announced. This had been the most serious washout of the great storm. Rumors said that the crossing was all quicksand, that the pilings had been driven forty, fifty feet down to find solid footing. I held my breath and took a grip on the armrest as the flatcar and engine rolled onto the trestle without slackening speed. In a moment we were across the Elkhorn and it was behind us.

After a few more miles I happened to have my head out the window, looking ahead, just in time to glimpse a white signpost beside the track. It came and was gone in seconds, but I had enough time to see that it was new and had a symbol painted on it. It looked like a raised fist with another fist pointing downward toward it. I was somewhat familiar with other such markers, symbols telling a locomotive engineer to sound his whistle for a grade crossing, or to reduce speed or watch for a siding ahead. As I was about to ask Mr. Boswell if he knew what it meant, I felt the brakes going on, and the train slowed to a full stop.

Mr. Boswell and one of the other men left the car and went forward to the engine. A few minutes later they were back with us.

"It's time," the detective announced.

"That clever lad who bosses the track crew set up a marker for us."

"The one that looks like two fists?" I said.

"A pair of couplings. It tells us to uncouple the flatcar at this point and shove it ahead. The engineer will give it a good push and then throttle back to see what happens."

Mr. Boswell chuckled.

"That crew boss! I'd like to shake his hand. He must have spotted the place where Kelly's boys unfastened the track. He put up a warning sign for us, right under their noses!"

"Gentlemen, if you will look to your priming, please, and conceal our weapons. Remember the plan. No matter what the temptation, sit perfectly still until I give the order — which may not be necessary. But if I say *shoot* I expect every man to hit his mark."

Earlier in the trip the detective had asked whether I was armed, and I showed him my Colt's pocket revolver, .32 caliber. He had smiled indulgently and handed it back to me. Now he patted my vest pocket.

"Best leave your cannon right there," he said. "Do not under any circumstance show it while the hoodlums are on the train or they might panic and shoot you. Unarmed you are quite safe."

Certainly, I thought. If this car turns into a shooting gallery, I'll be safe. Perhaps I'll hide behind my notebook. Oh, certainly safe.

The locomotive chugged forward again, pushing the uncoupled flatcar, letting it roll free along the track until it stopped rolling, then shoving it again. We were entering a stretch of track where the railroad had been cut through a series of low hills. Here the tall grass gave way to sagebrush. Exposed ledges of rock jutted out from the sand, evidence of Wyoming's legendary wind-storms. Kelly's men would have no trouble concealing themselves here, nor would they lack for blind corners and narrow passages with which to spring a surprise ambush. I went onto the front platform and stood on the step, leaning out to watch down the tracks.

This was the moment, no doubt about it. The engineer was still using the unattached flatcar as a probe, shoving it ahead of the engine and then slowing to allow the flatcar to roll a hundred yards ahead. When it slowed or stopped or began to roll back, he pushed it again. I watched with fascination, expecting at any minute to see the car and its load of railroad ties go diving off the tracks into the dirt. Or vanish into an arroyo because a trestle had been sabotaged.

Back inside the passenger car, Detective Boswell methodically filled his briar pipe and lit it. He relaxed against the seat as if he were an ordinary passenger enjoying the ride and watching the scenery.

"I don't know how you can be so easy," I called to him.

"Biding my time," he said. "Merely biding my time. Nothing to be accomplished by becoming nervous. I'll let the Kelly brothers get nervous instead."

Brothers? Plural? *Both* Kellys? Had Mr. Boswell let it slip that Kane Kelly was on board after all?

I returned to my seat and leaned forward to speak to him.

"For the sake of accuracy in my story, do you mean 'Kellys' to refer to the mob of men who work for Clifton Kelly and who seem to be waiting to attack us? I somehow inferred that by saying 'brothers' you meant that Kane Kelly *is* aboard this train."

Mr. Boswell smiled and enjoyed a long pull on his pipe.

"You need to relax, Mr. Pierce. All will be discovered soon enough."

Once again I found myself experiencing the sort of mental uneasiness that Mr. Boswell's criminal adversaries knew so well.

Was the prisoner on the train, and if so, where? Had the army already captured the train wreckers, and would we roll on to Laramie City unhindered? Perhaps he had arranged for a second train to follow us, perhaps carrying a posse and horses to pursue the villains. It was even possible that one of Mr. Boswell's Rocky Mountain Detective Association colleagues had already transported Kane Kelly to Laramie by means of the Overland Stage.

The train was about to emerge from the small range of hills. As we passed into the last shadowy cut, I felt the jolt of the engine striking the flatcar and sending it coasting forward. A moment after came the urgent blast of the engineer's whistle. The brakes went on, and we had to grab at the seats to avoid being thrown to the floor. Leaning out my window I could see the flatcar: a billowing cloud of dust marked where it had gone off the tracks and rolled down the embankment. It was still upright, and the load of ties was still in place.

From either side of the cars came a half dozen men carrying pistols and walking toward us with grim determination written all over their faces.

I rose to my feet and felt for my pocket revolver.

"Leave it where it is." Mr. Boswell's voice was quiet and reassuring. "Sit down and be calm."

CHAPTER 12

Two armed men entered our car, one at each end, menacing our group with pistols.

"They have a clever strategy, don't you think?" Mr. Boswell whispered, drawing on his pipe. "Coming into the car from both ends? If one of them pulls a trigger he'll hit the other one!"

We heard shouting and swearing from the car behind us, but our two "captors" said nothing. It was obvious they were waiting for their boss to finish searching the other car so he could come to this one. And come he did, but it was not rat-face brother Clifton. Instead, it was a burly blond gentleman carrying an absurd antique pistol, one of the double-barrel sort that became obsolete about the same time as the cutlass. He had all the look of a construction foreman, which he probably was.

"Which of you's Kelly?" he demanded. "C'mon gents, give 'im up and there'll be no trouble."

He raised the hat of the first man and peered into his face.

"You Kelly?" he said.

Detective Boswell removed his pipe from his mouth and dumped the ash out of the window before addressing this leader of thugs.

"And who might you be?" Mr. Boswell asked.

"Never mind that! Where's Kelly?"

"Do you mean Kane Kelly or Clifton Kelly? I wish you'd be more specific."

The twin barrels of the pistol came to bear on Mr. Boswell's vest buttons, but he remained as calm as a man giving directions to a kind stranger.

"Damn you! *Kane* Kelly!"

"I see. You tell me: where is Clifton Kelly?" Mr. Boswell asked.

"Near enough, near enough," snarled the blond man.

"Perhaps you need to summon him to identify his brother," the detective said. "I am reasonably certain none of your gang would know the infamous Kane Kelly on sight. In short, you don't know who you are looking for."

Mr. Boswell turned to me with a twinkle in his eye. "Or should that be *whom,* Mr.

Journalist? When you write this for the newspapers we do want it to be correct."

"I'm not sure," I said. "I've always been a little confused on where to put *who* and where to put *whom.*"

"Shut it!" the blond thug screamed. "Nobody puts it nowhere! Give up Kelly! Now!"

"You won't find him because you don't know what he looks like," said Mr. Boswell. "And you won't shoot because you're under orders not to. And because the instant you try to cock the hammers on that antique gas pipe, there will be six modern revolvers aimed at your heart. In your own best interests — and I am sincere in this — I suggest you collect your men before they accidentally shoot someone, take them forward, repair the track you unspiked, help get the flatcar back on it, and then leave. You could still get out of this without going to prison."

The blond man sputtered with anger. He looked from man to man in near panic, uncertain what to do next.

Adding to his frustration was the appearance of another member of the "rescue" squad, a stocky little fellow lugging a long pry bar, known to railroaders as a claw bar. No doubt they had used it when they pried loose the spikes from the railroad ties. The little man had no visible gun or knife, so I assumed he held onto the claw bar as his principal weapon, even though it probably weighed twenty pounds and was about as tall as he was.

"Boss says what's the holdup?" he squeaked. "Which one's the brother here? Boss says get a move on! Now!"

Detective Boswell leaned toward me and spoke in a whisper. He seemed as relaxed as a man making a comment about the weather. "I believe we have him!" the detective said.

"Meaning?" I asked.

"The 'boss' can be no one but Clifton Kelly. He has crept out of his hole and is now somewhere near the train. All I need do now is bait him into making a personal and illegal move."

"How do you know he's nearby?" I asked.

"Look at the messenger," he explained. "The sweat stains on his shirt and the dust on his face tell us he was one of the men who loosened the tracks. He hasn't been loitering back in the hills somewhere. And look at the weight of that claw bar — if he carried it more than fifty yards, I'm a Chinaman. No. Kelly has come out of hiding. His patience ran out, so he told this little

239

man to find out what was causing the delay."

The sputtering blond paced the length of the car once more before yelling at the little fellow with the big steel bar.

"He ain't here, I tell you! They oughta be some 'un here wearin' leg irons or handcuffs, but I tell you they ain't such a one in none of these cars. He ain't in the cars! Nobody's wearin' irons!"

"Mebbe a trick," squeaked the little man. "Mebbe they knocked him out. Drugs or somethin'. Didya think of that, you ox? Shake your tail, and find him!"

"Find him yourself, damn you! Find him yourself, or else get the boss in here. How the hell am I s'posed to recognize his brother! Hell if I know."

"More bad grammar," Detective Boswell whispered. "I wonder if there's a law against that."

There followed a quick series of developments, through which I was resolved not to leave Mr. Boswell's side, for I did not want to miss a single detail for the story I was going to write. The bulky blond man went storming toward the forward platform, sweeping the little man ahead of him. He jumped to the ground and I lost sight of him. But directly we saw "the boss" himself stomping toward our car with a pistol in his hand. The little squeaky fellow followed hot on his heels.

"Boswell, damn you!"

The detective looked out the window with mild interest and addressed Clifton Kelly.

"So," he said gently, "the famous Kelly Contracting Company has turned to train wrecking at last. Well, most of us knew it would happen sooner or later."

"Come down!" Clifton ordered. "Come down now or I shoot!"

Mr. Boswell signaled for me to follow and we descended the steps to the ground. There stood Mr. Clifton Kelly himself, the living stereotype of a pugnacious, blustering Irishman. Let him be wearing a comic green hat and waving a shillelagh and he could pose for an ale advertisement.

"Now, Boswell," he snarled, "surrender Kane or I'll kill you on the spot."

"Two problems with that," the detective answered. "First, you don't know that I have him. For all you know, I left him in Omaha to be taken by stagecoach to Fort Kearney. Second, if you shoot me in front of all these witnesses, you will quickly find yourself on trial for murder. Just like Kane. Your brother committed the murder of Charlie Madalone — there are a half dozen witnesses to the fact — he will go to trial for it, and that's an end to it. If you wish to follow him, then go ahead and shoot."

Kelly stamped his foot in frustration and waved his pistol menacingly. He looked about wildly, trying to keep track of his scattered forces.

"You stand here!" he hollered at us. "Both of you don't move! Or by God, I will shoot. Your game might go with these boys who don't know Kane, but I sure as hell do! Stand here!"

He told the small fellow with the large steel claw bar to guard us, then swung aboard the passenger car. There he angrily confronted each man in turn, knocking off hats and shouting his brother's name. Unsuccessful and further enraged, he repeated the procedure in the two other passenger cars and emerged on the back platform of the last car with a very red face and rage in his voice.

By this time most of his gang had come back to get further orders, having searched the cars themselves. In later interviews, several passengers told me how entertaining it had been to see one man and then the other go storming among the cars, shouting Kane's name and looking for handcuffs and manacles and asking each man — and in one case, an adolescent boy — whether they

242

were him. Now Kelly's henchmen were standing around in considerable anxiety, eager to be done with the program. They wanted to be gone before something else went wrong. Clifton Kelly, however, was far from finished.

He came storming back to us again, shouted "where is he?" again, but without any expectation of an answer, and demanded to know whether his mob had searched all the cars.

"Well," said the blond man with the double-barrel pistol, "all but the baggage car. We looked in the freight car."

"Morons!" he said.

The searchers had pushed open the door of the freight car during their hunt for Kane. Clifton holstered his gun and hoisted himself up into the car and began rummaging among the boxes and crates and bags. He kicked several sacks of potatoes, presumably hoping Kane was tied up in one of them. He tried the lids on several boxes and yelled "Kane! Kane!" at several other boxes before coming to the large crate Mr. Boswell had arranged.

I peered under the car and saw that Mr. Boswell's other predictions were coming true: on the other side of the tracks, two of the rogues had pulled down the crate of rifles, had opened it and discovered a dozen fine new Springfields. Like most males, they could not resist fondling the weapons and holding them to their shoulders to sight along the barrels. So now they were guilty of looting a train and tampering with US Army property. They were lining up plenty of work for the lawyers.

From the freight car Clifton Kelly yelled for the small fellow to bring the claw bar to him. The little man obliged, scurrying to hand the bar up to his boss. He turned from doing this and discovered the figure of Detective Boswell looming over him, fingering a pair of handcuffs he had half drawn from his coat pocket. Suddenly realizing that he was now without a weapon, the diminutive tough guy chose to withdraw from our company. He apparently had a sudden craving for exercise, for he went walking westward along the tracks at a vigorous rate of speed.

Clifton sweated and swore as he attacked the wooden crate with the claw bar. Being both too long and too heavy for the work, the bar made it an awkward and frustrating job.

"I heard about this special box of yours in Omaha, Boswell!" he shouted triumphantly, digging at the crate with the bar's flat end, "so you're not so smart! But I didn't think you'd do it! Even you, Boswell, you heartless bastard, even you wouldn't let a man suffocate in a box. Damn your eyes anyway! There ain't even any airholes! You've killed him!"

He managed, finally, to claw off one side of the crate, only to discover — a load of old mattresses. Totally oblivious to how foolish he looked, he went on shouting "Kane! Kane!" as he manhandled the mattresses out of the crate to search between and among them.

Detective Boswell leaned toward me and whispered, "Clifton's comedy show reminds me of that story of the boy who searched the coal shed for a pony! Finding a gunny sack of dry horse manure in the shed, he began digging through the coal yelling, 'Oh, boy! There's a pony in here somewhere!' "

Kelly made another search among the boxes and baskets before jumping down from the car. He confronted us with such frustration and anger that his face turned beet red and the veins on his pointed nose stood out.

"I've a mind to kill you, Boswell! There's those that'd thank me for it, and no mistake!"

I half expected Detective Boswell to draw

his own pistol at that point, as there was no predicting what the enraged Kelly might do. But without saying a word, and still smiling pleasantly, Mr. Boswell quietly pointed through the gap between freight car and baggage car. Kelly turned and saw his men fooling about with the army rifles. And he knew instantly what the repercussions of stealing army weapons could be. Pulling a revolver from his belt he fired a shot over their heads to get their attention. And get their attention it did. They stood up, still holding army rifles in their hands, looking like schoolboys caught with their hands in the cookie jar.

"Put those *back*!" Kelly raged. "Nobody told y'to go on a pillage! Put them back! Find Kane! Look under every car, one of you climb up and look on top! Boswell wouldn't leave him in Omaha. He's got him with 'im and you find *where*!"

He turned back to us, mouthing such oaths as I could not bring myself to copy down, let alone send to a family newspaper. Suffice to say that the labels he gave to those three men represented zoological impossibilities and anatomical absurdities. The outburst took its toll, however; the creative effort of formulating curses upon his henchmen left Kelly completely out of breath.

Continuing to show his amusement, Mr. Boswell now pointed toward the west. Clifton Kelly and I both looked in the direction indicated and saw a thin column of dark-gray smoke rising into the blue air. There could be no mistaking its meaning: an engine was approaching from the direction of Fort Kearney.

"Hmmm," said the detective. "Such dark smoke. You know, Mr. Pierce, I do believe it's one of the newer locomotives, the ones that burn coal. Coal makes a darkish smoke like that, especially when the engineer is pouring on the power. They are quite the coming thing out here in the West. Your local woodcutters may soon be out of work. And all these wood tenders on trains, they'll have to be converted to coal bins. Coal will be more efficient, of course. But I will miss the sight of a wood tender with all the cords of newly cut wood stacked tightly. There's an art to stacking firewood properly."

He seemed to muse for a moment and spoke again, acting as though he had forgotten the presence of Kelly.

"I was just thinking," he said. "You probably know how some of the engineers or firemen will stash a whiskey bottle in among the firewood — for those long drives, mind you — and I was thinking now they'll need to be careful their bottle doesn't get smashed in the shoveling of the coal! Wouldn't that be funny?"

"Jesus Mary Delaney!" Clifton shouted. "Will you shut up! Give Kane over! Now!"

If the approaching locomotive were not enough of a complication for Kelly, the little man who ran away came running back as quick as ever, so much out of breath he could only wave an arm in the general direction of the low hills ahead of the derailed flatcar and stalled train.

"What is it, man?" Kelly demanded. "Where've you been anyway?"

"Troops!" the man managed to squeak. "Top of the next rise! A mile, mebbe two! That's me for my horse and outa here, Kelly! Federal troops! To hell with you and your brother! Good-bye, Mr. Clifton Kelly, good-bye forever to you!"

He turned and he ran, presumably toward a remuda hidden in the hills, whereupon Clifton Kelly drew his larger weapon from its holster and sent a bullet that caught the small target somewhere below the waist.

The little man fell instantly, then raised himself to his knees. With howls and cries, he went crawling on, determined to distance himself from the whole scene. The newspaperman within me was stirred. I had an urge to follow him, to help him while I learned his story. What quirks, what caprices of history had brought this pitiful human to such an end as this? Ahead of him I could see nothing but the endlessly rolling hills of the Great Plains, the Great American Desert as Major Long's expedition labeled it. The wounded man was but a small speck in that vastness, a creature whose only value might be in the lessons his life story could teach to others.

"Poor little man. He'll have to wait for help, I'm thinking," Mr. Boswell said at my elbow. "Another check mark against Kane's brother. I hadn't counted on this. Now we have Kelly for attempted homicide. In addition to the other charges."

With his heavy revolver in one hand and dragging the steel claw bar with the other, Clifton rushed to the only unsearched car, the baggage van just behind the engine tender. For a moment I thought I saw a pale, frightened face peering out of the small window, possibly the mail clerk who had locked himself in the mail room. Clifton raged at the man who was trying without success to undo the latch on the baggage car door, pushed him aside, tried the latch himself. Finding it secured from within, he raised his revolver, assumed the classic marksman pose with gun arm extended and fired into the steel latch. The resulting ricochet of fragments of lead nearly nicked him and certainly frightened him. He let out another string of curses, most of them attributing canine characteristics to the inanimate bit of metal and fired again.

The second shot sprayed even more ricochet lead than had the first one. Clifton's response was to shove his pistol deep into its holster and take the steel claw bar in both hands. Again it proved to be an awkward tool for the work, being meant only as a means of moving rails on the ties. As his muscles began to tire, however, he managed to get the claw into the lock and, with a victorious yell, he wrenched open the latch.

Most of his henchmen had gathered near the car. Clifton put his shoulder to the door and slid it back, then jumped into the gloomy interior shouting, "Kane! Kane! Where are you?"

But again, no voice answered his. From my vantage point, all I could see in the shadows of the baggage car were trunks and parcels. Nothing big enough to conceal a Kelly, so far as I could tell. While his brother went on rummaging among the baggage, I looked to the west and saw that the telltale rising smoke of the new locomotive was no longer coming toward us. I inferred that it must have stopped on the siding Mr. Boswell had told us about. Two mounted soldiers were clearly visible, sitting motionless on a hilltop some half mile distant.

I pointed them out to the detective.

"Yes," he said softly. "I saw them. We may surmise that Lieutenant Wheeler decided against a frontal attack. I believe he has deployed his men around us. A clever officer. I would further assume that one or two of his scouts have already secured the horses and wagons that Kelly no doubt concealed behind the hill. I do believe, Mr. Pierce, that our fish is on the hook. All that remains is to bring him to the net."

"What about Kane Kelly?" I asked. "Is he on this train or not?"

"Shhh," the detective said, putting a finger to his lips. "Watch. Clifton is out of patience entirely."

And indeed he was. Mumbling great oaths that echoed inside the baggage car, he applied the ungainly long steel pry bar to the door of the mail compartment. The postal worker within shouted warnings against his breaking and entering, but this only inflamed the rogue like kerosene thrown on a fire. At last the doorjamb splintered. Clifton pulled the ruined door open, threw down

251

his pry bar and confronted the mail clerk. The clerk was genuinely frightened yet, as rehearsed by Detective Boswell, clutched a certain mail pouch to his chest as he cowered against the wall.

"No!" the clerk was heard to scream. "I know what you want, but you shan't have it! No!"

"What have you got there, damn you?" came the voice of Clifton Kelly. "What is it?"

"Federal property! The United States mail! You cannot seize it!"

Clifton hauled out his belt pistol and waved it beneath the clerk's nose.

"Why do I want it, you fool? Where's my brother?"

"I don't know. I don't *know*! I only know I have to deliver these depositions to Laramie City."

"Depositions? Against my brother? For his trial? Is that what you're saying? Speak!"

With Clifton's pistol shoved up his left nostril, the clerk gave up the information that the mail pouch did contain numerous witness statements to be used in Kane's trial.

Detective Boswell slipped me the wink and gestured for me to stay where I was. He leapt up into the baggage car with surprising nimbleness, where he stood nearly invisible beside the mail room door. I saw the glint of metal as he withdrew handcuffs from his coat pocket. None of the men on the ground moved. None of them knew what to do.

"Give it!" Clifton shouted.

Clifton wrenched the mail pouch out of the clerk's grasp, shoved his pistol back into his belt, and drew out a knife to cut open the locked canvas bag. There was a kind of manic triumph in his narrow face as he came out and stood in the open doorway of the car where he could get better light for examining his prize. He brought out letter after letter, tossing aside the ones that had no meaning for him and letting them drift down to litter the ground.

Detective Boswell quietly stepped up behind our frustrated quarry and pressed the edge of a handcuff into his spine. The fact that the detective had not drawn a weapon was not lost upon me. I felt nothing but admiration for the man.

"Please drop that knife to the ground," he said flatly. The knife dropped from Kelly's hand and clattered on the ballast.

"And put your hands behind you."

I heard the snap of the handcuffs and realized our adventure was nearly over.

253

"Clifton Kelly, I am arresting you on various charges, including theft and damage of property, theft and damage to property of the United States Army, train wrecking, attempted homicide on an unarmed individual, and seizure and illegal inspection of the United States mail."

He pushed Clifton to the edge of the doorway, and with one brawny hand he held the man's collar to steady him while he hopped down to the ground.

"Mr. Pierce," he said to me, "I see that you have your hands free. Would you be so good as to relieve this gentleman of his revolvers, and pat his pockets to see if he's carrying any other sort of knife or tool?"

I did so. When I backed away from this job, I had Kelly's two guns stuck in my belt, making me feel like quite a dangerous bandit myself. It brought to mind what someone had written about the invention of Mr. Samuel Colt's revolver — something to the effect of "God made men equal: Mr. Colt gave them equality."

Mr. Boswell raised his arm as a signal. The engine driver blew two sharp blasts with the train whistle. Immediately, the two mounted soldiers started into a trot toward us. Ahead of the engine and the derailed flatcar, coming along the rails toward us, there appeared a posse of track repairmen carrying claw bars, spike mauls, picks and shovels. And to say that they did not look happy when they saw the damage done by Kelly's cronies would be a gross understatement.

Some of the Kelly gang took to their heels in the opposite direction — one of them still clinging to a stolen army Springfield for which he had no bullets — only to be met by the same four resolute infantrymen who had already captured the horse guard. These young gentlemen in blue *did* have ammunition for their Springfields and looked as if they would be glad of some target practice should any of the train wreckers make a run for it. They herded their captives into the shade alongside the freight car and bade them take a seat on the ballast stones.

Lieutenant Wheeler rode up and dismounted to salute Detective Boswell.

"Another successful arrest, Detective," the lieutenant said. "My congratulations."

"A day's work, a day's work," said the detective. There was a trace of justifiable smugness in his demeanor.

"No doubt Mr. Pierce will find it rather dull material for his newspaper story."

Another man joined us. Mr. Boswell introduced him as Thomas Ring, the work crew superintendent for the Union Pacific.

"I had a hard time of it," he said, "holding the boys back, I mean. Until we heard your signal. Right now they're looking at the damage. What it'll take to put that flatcar back on the rails. Tell you one thing. If they had rope and a stout tree limb, some track wreckers would be twisting in the breeze. Alongside the killer of poor little Charlie Madalone."

"The question is," said Lieutenant Wheeler, "what to do with all these miscreants. I have nowhere to keep them. I can't spare enough men to take them to Fort Laramie."

"I have been thinking about that," said Mr. Boswell. "Let's go take a look at them, shall we?"

CHAPTER 13

How to write the story? This was going to make exciting reading for the papers, and without embellishments. In my mind I was already turning over some ideas for the opening lead. I wanted to get started on it right away, because as soon as the track was repaired, we would be on our way to Cheyenne or Laramie City, where I would be able to send it back to Omaha.

I withdrew to the top of the nearest hill where a small copse of wild plum offered a bit of shade. There I sat and wrote out my account of the journey and the train wreck, the confrontation and capture of Clifton Kelly. It was a simple and straightforward report, telling Omaha and Laramie readers what progress had been made in the Madalone murder case. In the idiom of journalism, I was sketching out the "what, when, who, how and where" of the matter.

The first four came to me automatically,

thanks to my having practiced on town council meetings and at the erection of new barns. The "where," however, had me chewing my pencil. How could I describe where we were when all of this took place? I attempted several versions of descriptive prose, none of which caught the essence of the place.

"Somewhere east of Fort Kearney" was true, but vague. "Somewhere west of Omaha, not too many miles past the Elkhorn River" was less vague but no less boring. I chewed my pencil again and studied the picture below me. Where were we, really?

About a mile west of the hill on which I sat, a locomotive waiting on the sidetrack was putting up a thin ribbon of smoke. Ahead of the other locomotive, the one that had brought us here, a gang of men were shifting the load of heavy ties from the tilted flatcar. Two men on horseback were guarding a mob of men sitting in the shade of a boxcar. Someone, either the engineer or the fireman, was inspecting the running gear of the locomotive. In either direction the parallel rails of track ran away to east and west and seemed to merge as they approached the horizon.

Where did the incident take place? The answer? On the "prairie." I smiled at the irony of the term, which was given to the place by early explorers who had never seen or even imagined such an empty tract of land. They didn't even have a word for it. So they used the French word, *prairie,* which means simply "meadow."

Some meadow, I thought. Behind me, before me, all around me the Great Plains with their desert of grass and countless hills seemed endless. And omnipotent, too, a living force of desolate land. The railroad made a tiny and terrifyingly fragile stripe across it, nothing more than a scratch such as a grain of sand embedded in a shoe sole might make on a ballroom floor. A few toy cars and a little toy engine sat on the rails while men the size of ants scurried here and there. For all of the human drama it represented — the murder and jealousy, revenge and rage, law and lawlessness — that little human scenario at the foot of my hill was lost in a sea of grass. If the land should will it to happen, the entire episode could be swallowed and erased in a matter of weeks.

So that was "where" the Kelly brothers ended up after all their bullying and murder, bribery and scheming. All it took to bring them down was one determined lawman. The lines from Shelley's poem "Ozymandias" came into my mind:

Round the decay
Of that colossal Wreck, boundless and bare
The lone and level sands stretch far away.

I settled for writing "a few hours out of Omaha" and quickly scribbled two copies, one to send to the *Herald* and one for the *Leader,* before rejoining Detective Boswell trackside. And to my surprise — one might even say amazement — standing beside the detective's deputies was none other than the murderer Kane Kelly, manacled hand and foot, looking rumpled and as abject as I had ever seen a man look. His brother Clifton, held in place by Jimmy Skroggs, looked equally defeated and despondent. Mr. Boswell was in conversation with Lieutenant Wheeler farther down the line of cars.

"Where?" I asked Jimmy Skroggs. "Where in the *world* did Kane Kelly come from? His thugs searched this whole train for him! I mean . . I thought maybe Mr. Boswell really had sent him by stagecoach! Was he on the train this whole time?"

The young man's face beamed with that big, infectious smile.

"We had him in the engine tender!" he said, sounding exultant. "Me and Constable Harris! Back in Omaha we got a wooden crate and buried it under the firewood, put a stool inside it for him to sit on. Oh, it was a real cozy little cell. Then we stacked more firewood in front of it. Say, he was safe as houses in there!"

In the wood bin.

In the engine tender, the whole time. And Detective Boswell, that scamp, had actually hinted at it while discussing coal-burning engines with Clifton Kelly. What an entertaining story this was going to be, once I had time to write the full account!

Seeing that the detective and the lieutenant were still in conference, I decided to go forward and gather more details for the next installment of my story. At the derailed flatcar the repair crew had unloaded the railroad ties. The men were now using the heavy timbers as levers and fulcrums beneath the car. One wheel at a time, they levered the car up and slid a timber under it to hold it, then levered it a few more inches, put more blocks under it, then did it again. They moved on to the next wheel and repeated the process, then the next wheel, until they had raised the flatcar to a level position sitting atop a crib made of railroad ties.

Lugging those heavy timbers and heaving and straining at the levers had taken its toll on the men. The crew was exhausted and ready to seek shade and rest. Their fore-man, Thomas Ring, was sympathetic.

"They're good boys," he told me, "but they're about wore out. And there's another foot or more to raise 'er before we can lever 'er onto the rails. The higher they build the cribbing, the harder it is t' get leverage on 'er."

"Couldn't you use the engine?" I asked. "Hook a chain to the engine and drag the flatcar back onto the tracks that way?"

"Well, I don't think so," Thomas Ring said. "The spikes are gone, y'see. We might end up bendin' the rail, or worse. No, as soon as the boys get some rest we'll keep on cribbin' 'er up. Slow and easy, that's the ticket. Just wish we had more men and muscle. Them ties weigh near at a hundred pounds each."

"I believe I can help with that."

It was the voice of Detective Boswell. He had come up behind us with eight of Kelly's employees — or I should say "former" em-ployees — three of them carrying claw bars and spike mauls.

"The lieutenant and I interviewed various of Kelly's gang and sorted them out," he explained. "These eight" — he indicated the bunch of workers with a wave of his arm — "would like the opportunity to work for you on repairing the track. In exchange for a ride home on the train."

"You're not arresting them?" I asked.

"It would serve no purpose," the detective said. "In fact, we're letting a dozen of them go. The other four of them have elected to walk back to Omaha. I've warned them not to commit any crimes or depredations along the way. Some of the rest of Kelly's boys will be going before a judge for assault on passengers and train wrecking. But these men you see here, the lieutenant and I have decided that they were little more than dupes. They were sucked into Kelly's ambush scheme without knowing what it was all about. I believe they are truly repentant. So, Mr. Ring. If you can use them, they are experienced. And with the Kelly Contracting Company out of business, they are unemployed."

"Done!" Mr. Ring shouted. "By God, we'll have the track fixed and that flatcar back on it in jig time! Boys! Lookit here! We got help! C'mon, time t'stop sittin' on your mittens and put 'em on. We got work to do!"

With four men on each lever and two on each cribbing timber, the flatcar was quickly raised level with the tracks. A brave volunteer crawled underneath to pry the steel rail into position and replace the spikes, and the thing was ready. Mr. Ring beamed with pride as we stood watching the men shift the flatcar a few inches at a time onto the rails.

"By the Great Gar," he said, "there's a crew for you! I'd like them fellows full-time, I would. They've 'bout got the last wheels on the rail now, see? There she goes!"

Sure enough, with a clang of flanges, the last set of wheels now settled onto the track. A dozen tired and sweating men put their hands on the flatcar and strained to start it moving toward the engine. The slight incline of the tracks was in their favor. After pushing the car a dozen yards, they were able to let go of it and let it roll free. There came a satisfying "clack!" when the couplings engaged, whereupon the men dusted their hands and grinned at one another.

"They done it," Mr. Ring said flatly. "Now we'll just reset those sleepers and get the rail spiked down good. Can't use the same spike holes, see? Spikes would just rattle loose again if we done that."

Detective Boswell and I left Mr. Ring and his crew to their work and returned to the passenger car. Clifton and Kane Kelly were handcuffed to a seat. They sat, docile and sad, under the eyes of Constable Harris and Jimmy Skroggs.

"Taking Clifton to Laramie with us?" I asked.

"No, we're not," the detective said. "That train on the siding ahead of us is on its way to Omaha with three cars. We'll stop there and transfer him. Then the constable and young Jimmy will take Clifton to Omaha and deliver him to the jail, where he will remain until he can be legally indicted. The soldiers retrieved his victim, that unfortunate little man whom he shot in the hip pocket. He will accompany them to Omaha, although he may have to stand up the whole journey. That individual is eager to give testimony about Clifton's various illegal activities. Like many small men, he has spent much of his life suffering indignities from bullies. Having Clifton shoot him in the ass was the final straw."

By the time Detective Boswell and Lieutenant Wheeler and Thomas Ring got everything sorted out, the bright rim of the sun was just touching the prairie's horizon. The lamps were lit in the passenger cars. I sat on a seat by myself, writing notes for the story I would compose. Sitting in the seat behind me, the detective puffed contently on his briar pipe.

"Here's to an uneventful ride into Laramie City, Mr. Pierce," he said.

"Amen," I replied. "Although I have found it awfully entertaining thus far. By the way, Mr. Boswell . . I meant to ask you. How did you come up with that trick of hiding Kane Kelly in the wood tender?"

He chuckled and drew on his pipe.

"I shouldn't answer that. It might cast a shadow over my character," he smiled.

"I won't tell anyone." I grinned at him.

"Well, as a lad back home, one of my chores was to cut limbs and logs into firewood billets, then stack them in an open shed. In order to teach me some rudimentary mathematics, my father would pay me by the cord. I soon figured out how to build cavities inside the pile, making it look like an entire cord, but involving somewhat less labor. Then one day I got an idea. The shed had a solid back wall. I stacked wood against that wall so that it made a cave. Big enough to hide a small boy. A small boy whose father might be calling for him with some job to be done. Such as weeding the turnips or collecting dry manure for the stove."

What an image.

In my mind I pictured a miniscule Detective Boswell, the man who never quit the chase, who didn't seem to sleep, the incorruptible and indefatigable detective, hiding from his chores. And tricking his father into paying him more than he should. What forces, do you think, could take such a mischievous rascal and make him into a model of civic responsibility? Why do we become who we become? Many philosophers have worried that question like terriers shaking a rag. Maybe there was hope that I would turn out to be more valuable than I imagined. Watching Mr. Boswell drawing on his pipe and reminiscing about his boyhood, I found more poetry jumping into my consciousness. This time it was Wordsworth:

Fair seed-time had my soul, and I grew up
Fostered alike by beauty and by fear.

This is the passage in which Wordsworth describes stealing a boat as a youth and feeling the fear, the terror of discovery and capture. Mr. Boswell understood those feelings well. And he uses them against his foes. Against the foes of our society.

The sun sank into the horizon at last. I scribbled away under the flickering, swaying lamp. I could not recall ever having been happier in my work than I was at that moment. I had a wonderful story, a colorful companion with excellent conversation, and I was on a modern railroad train speeding westward through those immense open plains. George Berkeley wrote, "Westward the course of empire takes its way." In those moments I felt I truly was part of an irresistible current of civilized mankind flowing out across the unsettled and primitive lands. We two had our roles to play: a detective promising honest settlers better law and order; and a journalist using the printed word to connect the West's villages and farms. Behind us would one day come a full legal system with elected officers, accompanied by an army of reporters establishing an entire network of newspapers.

I looked back at our murderer where he sat shackled to a seat, nodding in his sleep. His neck was already bowed in the posture of a hanged man. This, thought I, this is what the end of anarchy looks like.

CHAPTER 14

During the next four hundred miles we encountered no enemy except boredom. The night was long and cold. We twisted and hunched ourselves down into our coats and shivered, trying to sleep. Whenever the train stopped for wood and water, we descended from the car and walked forward in the dark to the engine, where we would stand in the heat coming from the engine.

On one of these occasions I rose, stretched my sore back and legs, climbed stiffly down the car steps and limped away into the brush in order to answer nature's call. Out there, beyond the circle of pale yellow light from the car windows, I experienced a moment of utter awe.

No words can describe midnight on the empty plains; the air was so transparent that one could see the curvature of the earth's horizon glowing distantly. Overhead, uncountable millions of stars formed a veritable glittering carpet. The heavens bent down to meet the curving horizon, giving one the sensation that he was standing beneath an overturned bowl of black glass spangled with silver dust.

Just after sunrise the train jolted to a halt again. This time it was a wood-and-water stop consisting of a windmill, a water tank on stilts and a squat log building in which there lived a lanky, bearded individual and his Indian wife. The bushy beard began to speak as soon as he saw us and, in thirty minutes of nonstop narrative, he let us know that he had been a mountain man, a fur trader and trapper, a famous scout and unappreciated explorer. Despite being of the strong and silent type (by his own modest admission), he knew travelers would want to know his story. Apparently he had not only shown Lewis and Clark the route to Oregon but had conquered the Sioux and pacified the Kiowa. He would still be trapping, had he not single-handedly decimated the beaver population of the Rocky Mountains from Canada to the Rio Grande.

This garrulous individual and his mute wife sold a breakfast to train passengers, their dining room consisting of an open lean-to or "ramada" beside the house wherein one found a huge coffeepot, a pile of sliced and dried apples, various unidenti-fiable cuts of dried meat and a basin of por-ridge. To partake of the porridge, one had to wait his turn: there were only four bowls and six spoons. Meals cost twenty-five cents each.

We stood around shivering against the morning chill while chewing on tough meat and leathery apples. True to the climate of the Great Plains, the chill was not to last. Within an hour of our departure from the breakfast stop, we were opening windows and leaning out to catch the breeze. The sun came up with unbelievable speed and turned the cars into ovens. As our car contained nothing but men, we agreed to shed our coats and travel in our shirtsleeves. One wag, a drummer on his way to sell gee-gaws to soldiers at Fort Laramie, suggested we might as well remove our shirts as well. He was met with a barrage of jokes about "the shirt off your back" and "lost your shirt," crude humor that provided some diversion as we continued rolling westward. And we kept our shirts on.

"Keep your shirt on" became a way of life for us in the days that followed. After our arrival in Laramie and the formal incarcera-tion and charging of Kane Kelly, events

271

moved so slowly as to try the patience of Job. Each day incorporated the same dull routine. I would rise, take my breakfast at the hotel, walk to the newspaper office in hopes of a story assignment; then I would walk to the courthouse to see whether Kane's trial had been scheduled. I covered a number of small stories, but not the sort that could be made interesting, even by the best of writers. The woman who took in washing had purchased a new patented wringer device; workmen laid the foundation for a new bank; an army representative was coming to town to buy horses.

There was action in Laramie City, but it didn't often make the news. The chief venue for excitement — but not of the reportable kind — was a tent bar Laramie's more respectable citizens called the Bucket of Blood Saloon. In actuality, its proprietors had named it The Belle of the West, a grandiose title considering that its walls were canvas stretched over a frame of logs. The saloon's name belied the ugly goings-on there. A fellow named "Jack" Lockke ran the place, along with two partners generally assumed to be Lockke's stepbrothers. These were "Deuce" Lockke and "Gyp" Thomas.

Detective Boswell and I were walking together one morning before the trial of

Kane Kelly. Our steps took us along First Street and past The Belle of the West.

"Never been in there," I remarked.

"Keep it that way," the detective said. "A den of thieves and murderers. I suspect it was the owners of that place who helped Kane Kelly in his original escape from jail."

"The local law . . they overlook its existence?"

"Mr. Jack Lockke *is* the law in this district, I'm afraid. Got himself elected Laramie town marshal. It is said — although I have not witnessed it personally — that he has a custom of strolling across the street to meet arriving trains. As passengers get off the train, he shows his badge and asks them to state their business in Laramie. Sometimes he finds one of those men who has bought land sight unseen, or with only a cursory inspection. Some speculators buy patented homesteads advertised in Kansas newspapers. But I think you know that. Anyway, when such an individual arrives and meets Lockke, he is invited to come to The Belle of the West for a free drink by way of welcoming him to Laramie. Once inside the saloon, the newcomer is prodded into revealing the details of his purchase. Should his land prove to be a piece of property Lockke would be interested in owning, one of the saloon gang professes an interest in seeing the place and offers to help the newcomer find it. One or more of Lockke's men accompanies the victim out of town to locate his property. And when they get there, Mr. Pierce, the victim comes to his end. He is shot or garroted and the property deed, warranty and other papers are turned over to Lockke and end up being registered in his name. So goes the story, at any rate. No proof. Only stories told by the mahogany polishers who hang out in the place."

My astonishment must have showed, for the detective gazed at my face and smiled wryly.

"Don't be too surprised. Laramie City's the edge of settlement, not the center of civilization. Witness our own adventure. Had the family of poor Charlie Madalone not engaged the Rocky Mountain Detective Association, Kane Kelly and his brothers would still be free to carry on their shoddy contracting business."

"But the citizens!" I protested. "There must be hundreds who would rise in anger if they knew there was such an operation going on."

"I believe everyone hopes someone else will do something. So long as it is not *their* ox being gored, they are content to let

Lockke go on day by day. Think of history, sir! Think back over the centuries to our European origins, when petty despots needed only a few weapons and a few loyal conspirators to set themselves up as lawgivers. I don't care which part of the Old Country you choose, nor which century, but you will find a history of such evil. Read some of the darker stories of King Arthur's enemies. Or those of the real Robin Hood. Ivan the Terrible, Genghis Khan, Vlad the Impaler. History is a veritable litany of human cruelty, murder and greed. Now it is we who are faced with it. Those same steel rails that carried us here to Wyoming also transported the outlaw plague. It spreads with the expansion of civilization like an epidemic."

"The other evening," I said, "you mentioned a desire to return to the East. Is it because of this lawlessness, then? I would miss your company."

Detective Boswell looked at me seriously for a moment, then smiled a friendly smile. In that smile I thought I saw a hint of something else . . loneliness, I thought.

"Because of the lawlessness? No. Shall I tell you? This is not for any ear but your own, mind you."

"Mum's the word," I said.

"I have bought a pretty parcel of land not far from Laramie. A good stream on it, plenty of trees and grazing. I intend to settle into ranching. Raise some cattle, perhaps breed some horses. Build a home. Chase chickens instead of outlaws."

"But your career in law!" I protested. "Could you really give up being a detective?"

"Between you, me and the fence post," he said, "I am not ready to be quits with it yet. I hope to run for the office of sheriff in Albany County. I believe I could do some good there. But I want a home as well."

"And going East? I'm sure you said you intended to go back east?"

"To Pennsylvania. There is a certain widow I told you about, she who assisted in the capture of the Kelly brothers. She is brave, intelligent, attractive and not without a fine sense of humor. If I can find the necessary money, I mean to visit Pennsylvania, locate her, and renew our acquaintance."

The murder trial of Kane Kelly was fair and thorough, proof that decency had gained a firm foothold in Laramie City. Witnesses to the shooting of Charlie Madalone were summoned, as were numerous other witnesses who could attest to Kelly's several attempts to avoid justice. Kane hired an attorney, but even a dozen attorneys would find their legal skills overwhelmed by the evidence against him. And this time, thanks to Detective Boswell, Clifton Kelly was not there to intimidate and bribe.

And so Kane Kelly was judged, convicted and sentenced. The judge and jury were not of the "Bucket of Blood" sort of men, but decent and honest. They were so decent and Christian, in fact, that they voted to send Kelly to prison rather than hang him. The courtroom audience included a contingent from Fort Steele who protested this decision, shouting for him to hang. They threatened to organize a necktie party at which Charlie Madalone's murderer would be the guest of honor.

What worried me was that Mr. Boswell might find himself among other law officers confronting a lynch mob. If he did, he would be defending the life of the very man he had worked diligently to incarcerate. But the talk of lynching proved to be nothing but talk. The judge's gavel pounded the desk, order was restored, and Kelly was returned to his cell.

I decided to stay in Laramie City. The air

was fine and clear, the population friendly and for the most part honest and ambitious. I wanted to linger a few years and see the growth of a new western town firsthand. The day after the Kelly trial I sent my story to the newspapers and returned to my custom of walking about town in search of more stories. I felt quite proud of the civilized way Laramie City had handled the trial. Suddenly even the mundane things seemed to show Laramie City was a good town and getting better. A new sidewalk, a fresh coat of paint on the church, a women's book club — these took on new importance to me. But there was still the grim side of town. I passed by The Belle of the West almost every day, and every day I wondered if I could find the courage to use my pen to expose the Lockke gang. The saloon was a filthy place and a murderous one, and someone needed to put an end to it.

Mr. Boswell was given fair and adequate compensation for his months and months of diligent, unrelenting pursuit of the Kellys. Seeing the detective receive his reward justified my faith in humanity. No sooner had reports of Kelly's conviction reached the Madalone family, than friends of the family raised a purse for the detective, a sum of money far exceeding the agreed-upon fee. A percentage of the purse went to the Rocky Mountain Detective Association, but the bulk of it came to Mr. Boswell.

"Well, Mr. Pierce," he said to me, "it seems I'll be going to Pennsylvania sooner than I expected!"

A short time later, Mr. Boswell was summoned to the Laramie bank where he discovered Lieutenant Wheeler waiting in the office.

"I have a check for you," the lieutenant said, smiling. "It is your share of a reward for recovering government property and taking actions leading to the arrest of the perpetrator."

"I have a check for you also," said the bank president. "The Union Pacific Railroad wishes to reward you for your help in the arrest of the track wreckers. They wanted it to be a public ceremony, but I convinced them that you are not the kind of man for such things."

Before many days had passed, I found myself standing on the platform of the Laramie station saying good-bye to Detective Boswell. He was about to mount the steps to enter the car that would take him on the first leg of his long journey to Pennsylvania.

He expressed some concern that he might

not be able to win the lady he sought. But I had seen the detective in action, and I had not the slightest doubt. I would wait in Laramie, write stories about patented washing machines and church dedications, and look forward to his return.

As things turned out, the washing machines and churches would have to wait. A bloodier saga soon unfolded, one that provided me with many inches of news copy. The growing city of Laramie was rapidly becoming populated with decent, hard-working citizens eager to realize the potential of the area's resources. The railroad brought more commerce. A fine, modern lumber mill provided jobs for men and materials for houses. A quarry was opened that would supply building stone, and there was talk of a possible coal mine being opened.

The entire town took on a civilized, pleasant appearance. Even the makeshift town of tents and shacks sheltering the ruffians and evil companions who had been associated with the end-of-track lifestyle gave way to brick and timber buildings, graded streets and platted town lots.

However, those bloody early days of Laramie had left one remaining scab, and it was The Belle of the West, also known as the

Bucket of Blood Saloon, on First Street.

The town held elections and chose a governing body to be led by a certain Mr. Edward Magnuson. He would have the title of mayor and would be chairman of the town council. It was clear from the beginning that the voters expected this duly elected, august group of men to clean up First Street. It was there that visitors descending from the arriving trains took their initial impression of Laramie City. Unfortunately, some of the city council members were corrupt, and others proved to be incompetent. Mayor Magnuson resigned in frustration.

It appeared that Jack Lockke and his stepbrothers would continue their reign of intimidation and murder. Everyone in Laramie City seemed to know how the gang used liquor and intimidation to rob newcomers, but no one, including the local law-enforcement officers, had the courage to step forward and stop it. The land transfers seemed to be legal, and who could show evidence that they weren't? Who would sign a formal accusation against the gang, what would be his proof, and what, exactly, would they be accused of? And so the Bucket of Blood remained open and the Lockke land steal went on.

It went on, that is, until a man known as "Hard Luck" Henry Jones happened to wander into Lockke's gun sights. Lockke met Hard Luck Henry at the train station and ushered him into the Bucket of Blood, where he plied him generously with liquor and flattery, until Henry began to brag about a rich timber claim he had purchased a few miles up the Little Laramie River. It would not be long, Henry said, until the town would need boards and beams from his claim. The way the town was growing, the lumber mill would pay premium prices for logs.

Having heard enough, Jack drew out his revolver. Calling for pen and ink, he ordered Henry to sign over his patent to the timber claim. Henry, however, refused to do so. Jack therefore shot him. The dying Henry pulled his own gun and returned the favor by wounding Jack in the arm.

Bleeding freely, Jack Lockke withdrew to seek the assistance of a woman he often spent his nights with, a "lady of the line" who had a shack just up the alley from the Bucket of Blood. While she dressed his wounds, Jack could not resist bragging how he had "killed his man" and spun out a tall yarn about a ferocious gun battle in which he stood his ground and emerged wounded but victorious.

In a later interview, this particular woman (who declined to be identified by name) revealed that Lockke's evening visit to her had represented the final straw. He burst into her lodgings dripping blood on the carpet and sat himself on the bed, where he continued to drip blood on the covers as he called for strong drink and bandages. He raved on and on, she said. He cursed and called her names, all the while blowing about his prowess with a pistol and his superior manhood in general.

The abuse did not surprise her, she said, since Lockke had a habit of abusing her. She had always been too afraid of him to protest, even when he slapped her. But this time was too much. She had wrapped his wound and washed the blood from his arm. He called her a filthy name and said she had done a slovenly job of it. Then he grabbed her by the throat and uttered terrible curses if she should ever reveal where he got the wound. To do so would mean painful and lingering death for her if she told anyone.

Other people already knew about the shooting; he had told her as much. Swearing her to silence and threatening her was simply another instance of Lockke dominating and intimidating a person for his own satisfaction. And she knew it.

As it happened — and let us not attempt to discover how — this wayward woman had recently developed a "working relationship" with one of the aforementioned town boosters. In fact, he was one of the same gentlemen who had organized the ill-fated town council to clean up Laramie City.

Jack Lockke left the woman shaken and angry and returned to the saloon to dispose of Hard Luck Henry's body. As soon as he was out of sight, she threw on a shawl and ran up the hill to the home of her new acquaintance, where she acquainted him with the facts of the case as told to her by Jack Lockke. Along with this information, she told what she knew about Lockke's land thefts.

By the greatest of coincidences, some honest citizens were meeting at the home of that same ex-councilman to discuss the resignation of Mayor Magnuson. These gentlemen were in no mood to look the other way as Lockke went on acquiring property by homicide. Hearing about the latest intimidation and shooting, they armed themselves and set out for the Belle of the West. Like the fallen woman, they were out of patience. If their town was ever going to become a garden spot of the West, they would have to get rid of the weeds. Rip them out by the roots and throw them on the trash fire.

I mentioned earlier that Laramie City was exploiting the local pine forests and that the local lumber mill was prospering from the sale of planks and timbers. One example of same was a house under construction up at the end of First Street. The framing was in place from floor joists to the heavy rafters, along with a number of stout ropes used to hoist beams into position.

The civilian posse armed themselves and rushed the Belle of the West. With the advent of the posse, walls were shredded, chairs broken, tables overturned. Customers fled in panic, leaving Jack Lockke and two of his henchmen behind. This evil trio was caught red-handed with the body of Hard Luck Henry — a sort of ironic *habeas corpus* — and the posse lost no time tying them up and accusing them of murder.

Jack and his two confederates were conducted to the aforementioned house under construction. And the posse did not take them there in order to discuss the advantages of frame construction over that of a tent saloon. Three of the carpenters' ropes were commandeered and slung over the high rafters. Two stepladders and two planks were assembled into a scaffold. Before long, three outlaws were swinging gently in the Wyoming evening, bathed in the red glow of the burning Bucket of Blood.

It was said that Jack Lockke's final words consisted of a request that his hangmen remove his boots prior to his execution.

"Do it for my mother," he said. "She always said I'd die with my boots on."

We did not realize it at the time, but the conviction of the Kelly brothers and the lynching of Jack Lockke and his henchmen marked a turning point in the history of the West, at least in our part of it. Laramie City became pretty tame after that. Various unassuming citizens cautiously took seats on the city council. Taxes were levied for the improvement of streets and services, including a fire department. It was still a tough town in a tough territory; however, a semblance of civilization had taken hold, and never again would bullies be allowed to hold sway.

As for myself, I was called to Cheyenne to accept a desk job with the Cheyenne *Leader,* a position offering more salary but far less interesting working conditions. My responsibilities grew. The owner/publisher "took a shine to me," as we used to say, and one day I finally realized that he was surreptitiously preparing me for the editor's desk, where I could grow fat and lazy and spend my life watching reporters having all the fun.

As soon as diplomacy would permit, therefore, I began to apply to various newspapers farther south, papers in Denver City, Pueblo and distant Santa Fe. I knew some other newshounds who said that east was the way to go — out onto the prairie to such towns as Dodge City, Abilene, Ogallala and Topeka, where "things were a-poppin'," but my adventure with Mr. Boswell had given me enough of the plains and prairies to last me a while, and I wanted to live where I could see the mountains. No, I would head for Denver and the Colorado gold camps and go back to being a stringer for any newspaper that would have me.

During the following years I used Mr. Boswell's name to gain access to various members of the Rocky Mountain Detective Association, men who were invaluable as inside sources of information about the criminal element of the West. I'm proud to say that I made the acquaintance of General Cook himself, the founder of the detectives. The saga of General Cook's campaign against crime could fill several volumes. I understand he is now writing his memoirs, which should prove to be very popular with readers interested in the West.

Detective Boswell and I lost contact with one another, but I read in the wire exchanges that he had eventually returned with "the lady in question" and had taken up ranching in the vicinity of Laramie City. He was elected sheriff of Albany County, and was later chosen to be the first warden of the new territorial prison at Laramie. I could well imagine him in these two administrative positions, and had no doubt that he would do a capable job; however, I could not imagine him giving up the days of pursuit without regret. We had shared freezing nights together and gone for days without a decent meal, yet there was an excitement and sense of adventure to our hardships that could never be found sitting at a desk.

During my subsequent travels, whether I was searching for stories in the southwest or along the Rocky Mountains, whenever I came across a crew of men building a road or laying rails, I would stop and watch them a while and remember.

ABOUT THE AUTHOR

Winner of the Colorado Seminars in Literature Annual Book Award for *Prose and Poetry of the American West* and the Charles Redd Award for *Following Where the River Begins,* **James Work** has published sixteen books. His Five Star novels include six books in the Keystone Riders series and two literary mysteries. He won the Frank Waters Southwest Writers Award in short fiction and served as president of the Western Literature Association as well as executive director of Colorado Seminars in Literature. At Colorado State University he was professor of Western American Literature and cofounded the university's program in nature writing.

The employees of Thorndike Press hope you have enjoyed this Large Print book. All our Thorndike, Wheeler, and Kennebec Large Print titles are designed for easy reading, and all our books are made to last. Other Thorndike Press Large Print books are available at your library, through selected bookstores, or directly from us.

For information about titles, please call:
(800) 223-1244

or visit our Web site at:
http://gale.com/thorndike

To share your comments, please write:
Publisher
Thorndike Press
10 Water St., Suite 310
Waterville, ME 04901